Satan's Spawn

B. L SWERN

ISBN : 979-8-9909151-0-7

Book Cover design by Disturbed Valkyrie Designs

Editor: Indie Editorial LLC

My amazing PA: Bethany Smith

First edition: August 2024

Dedication

To all the feral book sluts who run off of red flags, masked men, and chain me up daddy vibes. You are welcome!

Sorry, Mama, you tried!

Trigger Warnings

Your mental health matters. Before moving forward, please read below triggers. If any of the below affect you, please do not move forward with the book. Protect your peace!

This book contains very dark triggering situations, such as depicted rape—please proceed with caution and self awareness. There are graphic details of gore, torture, knife play, gun violence, PTSD, alcohol, threats, break-ins, drugged, set up, harassment, stalking, sexual assault, kidnapping, fighting pit, death, forced proximity, animal death (crows), gruesome description of dead bodies, blood. There are sexual kinks including knife handles, being tied up, ball gagged, jingle balls, anal plug, forced pleasure, masked men.

Playlist

S on of a Sinner — Jelly Roll

Bad girl — Avril Lavigne ft. Marilyn Manson

Ya'll want a single — Korn

V.A.N — Poopy and Bad Omens

Like a Villain — Bad Omens

A Bar Song — Shaboozey

Beautiful Things — Benson Boone

Wild Ones — Jessie Murph and Jelly Roll

Bulletproof — Nate Smith Feat Avril Lavigne

Morally Grey — April Jai & Nation Haven

Can You Feel My Heart — Bring Me The Horizon

Skin and Bones — David Kushner

Lovin On Me — Jack Harlow

Too Sweet — Hozier

Just Pretend — Bad Omens

Best for me — Joyner Lucas Feat. Jelly Roll

Prologue

REGAN

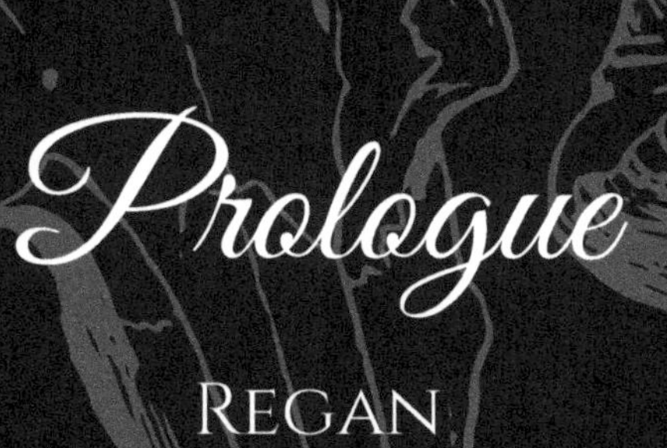

Chains rattle against the walls. A musty smell fills the room, making me want to gag.

Drip... Drip... Drip...

The sound fills my ears like white noise, growing louder and louder. I can't shut it off.

My head is pounding, aching more and more by the minute. Eyes opening slowly, looking around the room, I realize I am chained to a wall. My heart races. I try to get my hands free of the chains, but they are too tight. I can feel a deep cut in my side throbbing with liquid running down my hips and legs, the smell of copper hitting my nose.

Memories slip in one by one. The asshole cut me—no—he stabbed me. That was my doing. He warned me to shut up, but I don't take orders very well. Because

I do not know how to keep my smart-ass mouth shut, he launched at me and actually did it this time.

I try to pull on the chains to see if they give, but they don't budge. I can't scream with the gag in my mouth. No one will hear me, anyway. No one here cares.

Tears roll down my face as I realize just how royally fucked I am. Will I even live this time? I have to get the fuck out of here.

I hear footsteps coming and my body shakes. This is a game for him. He lives and breathes to see me in pain. It fuels him to see terror in my eyes. It is all about control and how far he can push me before I break and surrender to him. He has beat me, choked me, and raped me, but never has he attempted an act where it would kill me, except for this round.

The door swings open, hitting the wall behind it. He comes into view with a sinister grin on his face.

"Hello, little dove. Have you missed me?" He closes the space between us, stroking his finger down my cheek, and licks my face. I shudder. "Since you were a good little dove, I will let you out early. We have an important dinner tonight. Your dress is on your bed. You need to get yourself stitched and cleaned up." He unchains me from the wall, and I fall to my knees, yanking the gag out of my mouth.

I glanced around the room for anything to help me. This is my chance to get away. I have to run. To be truly safe, I need to get back home to the Wolves' protection. I can't stay and live out my dream to be free while he is my prison. Spotting a knife as he turns his back, I grab it and stand. He turns back around, and I shove it into his chest. His darkening eyes lock with mine. Shaking the image, I spit in his face and run out of the room, not looking back because I know stabbing him won't keep him down, and I need to get out of here.

"You can fly, my little dove, but I will find you. You are mine," I hear him yell.

I don't look back as I continue running. Finding keys on a table, I grab them and dart out to the front of the house. I trip and fall over a step. My body is throbbing, but I refuse to be weak.

I can't be weak ever again. Getting up, I run toward the car, climbing in and wincing at the pain as I put the vehicle in drive, speeding away. The need to get home intensifies. I weave through the traffic like a raging maniac toward my school to get to my dorms. There are too many people around; he knows better than to make a move.

I pull to a stop and race out of the car, rushing through the doors, not caring that people are staring at me like a crazy girl who has lost her mind. I know I don't have much time; he is coming for me. I can feel it. The only thing pushing me is this pure fear that he would appear behind me at any second.

Once I get to my dorm, I grab my suitcase that I had already packed under my bed. I strip off my bloody clothing and place a temporary bandage on my wound. Throwing on fresh clothes and my favorite pair of Vans, I also put a hat on to shield my face. I wince at the pain that shoots up my side, but I can't stop to stitch it up until I am far enough away.

Sucking in a breath, I keep going. Adrenaline pumping through my body, I can't slow down now. I grab my backpack that holds my wallet, documents, charger, and things I know I will need for the drive back. Everything was prepared to leave because I knew eventually he would kill me. I just needed to find the right moment because every step I made, he knew. Throwing on my backpack, I grab my keys, slide my phone in my back pocket, and hurry out the door. My heart rate picks up as I scan the area to make sure he didn't catch up to me. I reach my truck, throw my suitcase and backpack in, and take off. God, if you are real, please let me get out of this. Please don't let him catch me.

I have been driving for six hours, and I know I need to stop and rest. I'm terrified. If he finds me, I know he'll kill me. But if I don't stop, I will fall asleep behind the wheel and it will all be for nothing. As I pull into a motel, putting my truck in park, I reach over to a secret compartment in my truck, scan my thumbprint, and pull out a new license plate. My father had all of us hide a spare in our vehicles in case anything happened. I never understood why. Hopping out of the truck, I scan the area to make sure I don't have anyone following me or on-lookers staring, then switch my license plate quickly.

Now that I am in wolf territory, I know he won't cross over. I don't know why, but I do know he forbade me from going anywhere near the border. He gave me a small glimpse of freedom to continue attending school, but I never crossed over to see my family and friends because I knew I would get my sliver of freedom taken away and punished. I should have crossed over a long time ago, before it became this bad.

Opening the door to the motel entrance, a bell rings. An elderly woman walks out of a room behind the desk with a smile on her face; it falls as she scans me up and down. I know my hair is sticking up everywhere, my body is dirty, and I probably smell. Luckily, I changed out of my bloody clothes, or she would really be looking at me like I am crazy.

"Hi, dear. How may I help you?" She plasters on a smile again, but her eyes continue their perusal of my disheveled appearance.

"Hi. I need a room for one, just for the night." I unzip my backpack as my hands start to tremble. Now that my adrenaline is easing away, the pain in my side is becoming more and more present. I grab my wallet and hand her my ID.

I look out of the window as she is typing my information into the computer. My anxiety kicks up, tapping my foot as I stare out the window, watching for any figures to appear.

"Here is your room key. Your room number is twenty-five. Check out is at 11 a.m." I hand over my card, paying for the room, and place my ID back into my wallet.

"Dear, are you okay? You're trembling. Do I need to get you some help?" A worried look spreads across her face as she observes me once again.

"No, thank you. I'm fine, just a little cold and tired. Thank you for your help." I plaster on a smile, grabbing my card and bag and walking out the door.

Approaching my room, I slide my key into the top lock until I hear a click, opening the door. Rushing in and slamming the door shut, I turn the top lock and secure the deadbolt. Walking over to the window next to the door, I peer out to make sure no one followed me. The parking lot is empty, except for a few cars and a couple walking their small dog. My body remains shaking, terrified, on the verge of an anxiety attack. So, I shut the curtains, blocking my view of the outside world to provide somewhat of a relief. Trudging over to the lamp sitting on top of the bedside table, I turn on the light, noticing a queen-sized bed with a white, fluffy comforter that is calling my name to sink under.

Looking down at my hands, blood stains my palms and fingers. Striding to the other side of the room and entering the bathroom, I flip on the light. There is a granite countertop with a sink and a mirror on the left side. Peering into the mirror, my hair is sticking out like a crazy person, and my face is covered in grime. No wonder the lady asked if I was okay. She must have thought I was part of a murder or coming out of a nuthouse by the way I look. There is a walk-in shower straight ahead that is screaming at me to get my ass inside. Turning the knob to hot and peeling my clothes off, I stand under the scalding hot water.

After what feels like an hour just standing under the streaming water, I grab a washcloth hanging outside of the shower and squirt hotel soap onto it and clean off the dried blood and dirt. Looking down, the evidence of my torture disappears into the drain. Washing my hair next, the smell of ginger and lemon fill my nostrils as I massage my scalp. After the shampoo and conditioner are washed out, I turn off the water, step out, and wrap a fluffy towel around my body.

Rummaging through my bag and grabbing my hairbrush and toothbrush, I get to work on my knotted hair and brush my teeth.

Snatching my first aid kit, I pull out alcohol, a needle, and thread. I pour the alcohol on my wound, causing me to wince as the burn heightens. I thread the needle and start stitching.

Once I finish, I get dressed and walk over to the bed, sinking under the covers. Tears start to roll down my face. How did I get into this position? Running for safety to the very place I wanted to get away from. I stare at my phone; I need to make the call. It is the only way to ensure my survival, but I keep hesitating. I take a deep breath and dial out.

"Dad, I am coming home. You were right, and I failed. I guess you are getting what you wanted."

Chapter 1

The Wolves

Seth

When you are the son of the highest ranked Elder, you have high expectations placed on you. Whether you want to be part of the pack, you have no say in your future. Becoming a part of the wolf pack has always been my father's demand of me. He always told me that "you either become part of the pack or you're nothing." There are bright sides to being part of the pack. One, you have money, and you don't run out of it. Two, you are at the top of the chain and feared. Three, not even the law can touch you, mainly because you control them.

Just because you're born from the member of the pack does not mean you will remain a member. You have to prove that you are worthy. In my case, I have to prove myself to my father and the Elders.

You can be with whomever you choose, as long as it is not someone associated with the Snakes.

Women cannot join the trials, but they work for the pack in businesses, hospitals, or stay at home with the kids. We are not allowed to speak about the trials, assignments, or secrets with them, but they are not stupid. When their husbands come home bloody and wounded, they are not to ask questions. They tend to them to make sure they heal.

To become part of the pack, you are put through initiation trials. They don't tell you what the trials are, but growing up with the Wolves, you have an idea. You either live and become one of them, or you die a disappointment.

Not all initiates make it through the trials. The trials are made to weed out the weak. You either pass the trial or you are disposed of. Why would anyone want to join, knowing that if you do not pass, you die? It's the power, respect, and loyalty you gain. Every man wants that, and if they say they don't, they are lying.

Once you make it through the trials, you are branded with a wolf tattoo across the chest. You are also given a ring to wear. When your tattoo is covered, that ring symbolizes that you're one of them.

One night, my father came back from an assignment. He was bloody and bruised, with a ghostly look on his face. Without a word, he walked into his office and slammed the door. He didn't come back out for hours. I didn't dare to disturb him by asking questions, knowing whatever had happened may cause him to lash out. The look he had haunted me.

I didn't want to live my life with that look, with the feeling of hollowness, dead inside.

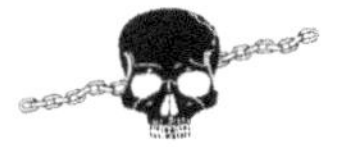

My older sister Bailey barges into the room as I'm playing Call of Duty. "Seth, we are going to a party. Get dressed—you have five minutes."

"Bailey, I'm not going to a damn party. Go by yourself or take one of your annoying friends with you." I continue to stare at the screen, twisting and turning my controller. Finally, I have a day off from work, and all I want to do is relax. I've been working my ass off because I need to move out of this house and finally open up my club that has been in the works.

"Please. Please. Please, Seth. Daddy won't let me go unless you go. You would think being twenty-two-years-old, I could do whatever I want, but not under this roof. Just this one time, and I won't ask ever again. Pleaseeeeeee," she whines, tugging on my arm. Fuck, I just got killed.

Standing up from my bed, I toss the controller. "Fine. I'll go if that means you'll shut up." I head into my bathroom to get cleaned up.

Pulling up to the party, which is hidden in the middle of the woods, I sigh, putting the truck in park. There is music blaring, people making out, and a huge bonfire blazing in the center. I need a beer. As we hop out of the truck, I spot Regan. Her hair is pulled back in a ponytail, and she is wearing a tank top and shorts that barely cover her ass—so simple, but so beautiful.

"You know, the two of you keep dancing around each other, but we both know she's going to get hurt in the end." Bailey leans up against my shoulder, staring toward Regan.

"What is that supposed to mean?" I ask, shoving her off my shoulder and turning to face her.

"What I mean is, you're two years older than her. She is eighteen, young, and getting ready to go to college. You, however, are expected to join the trials for the Wolves any day now. We don't know how the trials are going to end up. You live or you die. If you live, you'll have enemies that'll come after her to hurt you. Do you really want to put her through that?" She narrows her eyes at me, trying to give me the "big sister" talk.

"Since when is it your place to speak about my business, Bailey? You know nothing about the Wolves or my situationship. Who's to say if I am going to join the trials? Back off." My lip curls.

"Seth Joshua Kingsley. You have no say in that matter, and you know it. Get off your high horse. Let the girl go. She's good, better than any of us."

"How are you giving me advice when you can't even hold a relationship? You fuck around and hop on every dude that crosses your path. Tell me again how that's working for you." I spit back at her, cringing as soon as the words leave my mouth.

"Fuck you, Seth." She shoves past me, and she runs off toward a group of girls.

After several hours, the party starts to die out. Regan had gone back home with her friends, and I search the area for Bailey, but I can't find her anywhere. She must have run off with her friends or another fling. Spinning back around, I get into my truck and head home.

The next morning, I wake up to pounding against my bedroom door. Rubbing my eyes, I slide out of bed, swinging my door open.

Before I can open my mouth, my father is in my face. "Where the fuck is Bailey, Seth?" He walks past me, searching the room.

"I don't know. Why would she be in here?" I stare at him like he's lost his damn mind.

"Because she never came home. No one has seen her since the party. You fucking left without her." His fist flies, hitting me in the jaw, then rushes out of the room, bringing his phone to his ear.

It's been three weeks, and my sister hasn't come back home. We have search parties out in the woods, and have spent countless hours reviewing street cameras for any clues on where she may have gone. We haven't had any luck.

As I'm in my father's office reviewing footage, we hear a scream from my mother. Rushing out, I freeze when I find her on her knees, screaming and sobbing. There's a head on the floor, with hair covering the eyes. I can't breathe. My heart is pounding out of my chest—it can't be.

Averting my eyes to my father, I observe him shoving a piece of paper in his pocket. His fist goes flying into the wall, causing a massive rift. My body goes numb. This is all my fault. If I wouldn't have had that fight with her and spit vile venom her way, she would have been home safe with her family.

We have a beautiful funeral for her. Twenty-two-years-old, and she didn't have the chance to live her life. She didn't have a chance to travel, have a career, or have a family of her own. It was ripped away from her. Her choices were ripped away from her.

My father lost his humanity that day. She was his everything. She brought out the sunshine on gloomy days. He lost his princess, his daddy's girl, the one thread that kept him sewn tight. I haven't seen a smile on his face since. He's pushed me harder to join the trials, and I've stopped arguing with him.

He lost his favorite child and all that remains is a disappointment who couldn't keep her safe. So, I train. Every day I meet with him and Oliver, a family friend who owns a ring shop, and they teach me how to fight properly. They teach me survival skills and how to shoot a gun, making sure I hit the bullseye each time. If I don't, I get the butt of the gun slammed into my temple.

I'm pretty sure my father is taking out all his aggression and anger on me while we spar. Each day that we train, I have a busted eye or lip. One day, he loses control, slamming his fist into my ribs, swinging toward my head until Oliver throws him off of me. I let him. I deserve it.

Oliver has taken over my training, since training with my father had turned into more of a punishment than anything. He's one of the best fighters I've ever seen. He's flipped me on my back, knocking the wind out of me several times, as well as handed me my own ass more times than I can count.

When I'm not training, I am working on the final steps in pinpointing the location for my club to reside. I have to keep my mind busy. When I'm not busy, the shadows creep in, pulling me toward the darkness. I am struggling to keep hold of what is left of my humanity.

For my sister, I will join the Wolves. I'll let go of the one thing I actually care for. I will pass the trials and seek her killer, claiming our family's revenge.

Maybe I'll finally gain respect from my father. Maybe my mother can finally rest at night peacefully. But for me, there will never be peace. Not when I let down the one person who saw who I really was.

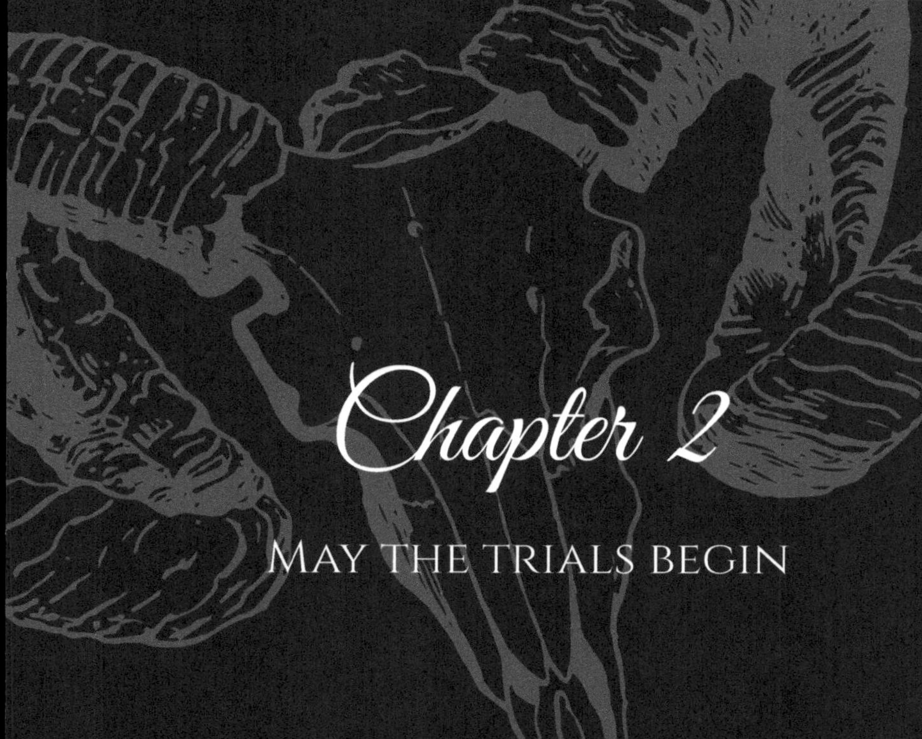

Chapter 2

MAY THE TRIALS BEGIN

Seth

Four Years ago...

"Come on, man, it's one party. You never get out, and you always have a stick up your ass. You need to let loose for one damn night." Cole has a stupid smirk on his face. Cole and I have been best friends since we were practically born. Our fathers are both the Elders of the pack and best friends. "Plus, I need an easy lay tonight before our trials start."

"Alright, let's go before I change my damn mind." I climb into my truck and start the engine. Cole connects his phone to Bluetooth and blares *Down with the Sickness* by Disturbed as I rip through my dirt driveway. We pull up to an old warehouse on Elm, and it's fucking packed. Trucks and cars are spread out everywhere, with people sitting on the back tailgates and walking toward the entrance of the warehouse.

It took me a solid ten minutes to find a place to park. I slam the door as I get out of my truck, scanning my surroundings. Damn, there are too many fucking people here. I can't stand the annoying ass squeals from the females with the fake tits, lip injections, and dressed like what they think someone will fall in love with them. When, in reality, they look like any other easy lay we could fuck and throw away when we are done. Maybe that's just what I need—a quick, easy fuck.

Cole and I make our way to the warehouse. The lights are cut off, allowing strobe lights to fill the space, and the music is so loud it is almost impossible to speak to one another. People are having the time of their lives, grinding on one another without a care in the world. It must be nice to not have impending torture and possible death hovering over their heads, or unattainable expectations of the Elders. We make our way to the bar and grab a whiskey each.

Leaning against the bar, I scan the crowd, and my eyes land on her. Regan fucking Dale. She's in a skimpy short, tight dress that hugs her curves in all the right places, including that juicy ass. Her red hair is spilling down her back in curls, and her plump lips are shining from the gloss, and crystal blue eyes are hypnotizing. We lock eyes and she instantly flips me off, pushing through the crowd to get as far away from me as possible. I had one chance with her and I fucking blew it.

I have known Regan since we were kids. She was always sassy as hell, always wanting to hang out with the boys. But of course, being two years older, we didn't want a little redhead following us around. As we got older, we played in circles, trying to get each other's attention, but also playing hard to get. One night at a party, she was extremely drunk and confessed her feelings for me. Like the dumb ass I was, I told her she couldn't handle the Wolves and that I would never be caught dead with a Dale. After that night, I made it my mission to make her life hell. I dragged her through the mud because I didn't want her to be associated with the Wolves.

I couldn't have her be turned into a piece of meat that was thrown away once she was done being fucked and used. I wasn't good enough for her then and am certainly not now. But I have always loved her. Sometimes, you have to become someone's Satan to protect them. That doesn't mean I wouldn't burn this world down to make sure she is safe—even if it means I walk through the fire and burn myself.

"Drink up, stop gawking at Dale, and let's go hunt for some nice cunt tonight." I shake my head, down the whiskey, and push off the bar. We head through the crowd, looking for our prey for the night. Cole quickly grabs a bleach blonde with a busty chest around the waist and starts grinding on her. Her friend looks over and starts walking in my direction. Once she is close enough, I grab the back of her neck and forcefully press my hungry lips against hers. She starts grinding on me, and I slide my hands down, gripping her waist.

Out of nowhere, the strobe lights are cut, and it goes pitch black. Suddenly, a chain wraps around my neck, with a bag pulled over my head. As the chains begin to cut my airways, my hands latch on, trying to get them free to pull over my head. Before succeeding, an object hits me so fucking hard in the stomach that I stumble to the ground, slamming onto my knees. There is a sharp prick to my neck, and then everything fades out as I lose consciousness.

Groaning as I slowly come to, I realize I'm chained and hanging by my arms above my head. I try to maneuver to slip my hands free, but the chains dig deeper into my wrists, cutting off circulation. There's no use. The damn bag is still suffocating over my head, and it smells like complete ass. I hear chains hit the wall, signaling that I'm not alone. I wonder if it's Cole.

The bag is yanked off my head, and my vision comes back in blotches. There are three figures standing in the room with red hoodies and what appears to be wolf-like masks on.

"Welcome to the trials. I hope you had a good time tonight. Buckle up, now is your front seat to hell." One of them walks up to me and punches me right in the jaw, snapping my head to the side. Bitter copper floods my mouth.

Spitting the blood on the ground, I lift my head with a sinister grin. "You hit like a bitch. Is that all you got?"

The masked wolf tilts his head to the side, grabs a bat, and hits me first on the leg and then the ribs. "Your first trial is to see if we can break you. Can you handle the pain or will you crumble? Will you beg for your mommy and daddy, or will you take it like a good little pup?"

I hear a cry of pain and look over to the other wall and realize Cole and Cade are there. They are both getting their fair share of beatings by the other two masked Wolves. After what feels like days, but is only several hours, we are unchained and dropped to the floor. The three Wolves turn and walk out of the room, heading up the stairs, leaving us broken in a pool of our own blood. I am pretty sure they broke my ribs and leg.

"You look like shit. Hopefully, that pretty face of yours comes back, or else you may need to wear that wolf mask permanently if you make it through your trials." I rotate my shoulders, wincing at the movement, as my eyes roam to where the voice had come from. It was Cade, who looks even more rough than I feel.

"Coming from someone who has a busted jaw, swollen eyes, and a five head," I say, as I'm patting my jeans for my phone. "What the hell are we supposed to do now, considering we don't have our phones?"

"For starters, we can get off our knees and get the fuck out of here and worry about our phones later," Cole grumbles, shooting a glare in our direction.

Grunting, we drag our bodies across the floor toward each other. Cole and Cade manage to get to their feet, grabbing me under my arms, lifting and providing me with support. We slowly climb the stairs, cringing and grunting at the pain.

We open the door at the top of the stairs and look around. We realize we were in the church's basement—classy. It's pitch black, but I can smell the fresh smoke from when the candles were blown out.

We shuffle out of the church, finding Cole's truck parked in the gravel. Slowly, we make our way, stopping at the front of the truck. Cole's keys are laying on top of a note.

You have passed your first trial. Keep your eyes and ears open for what is to come.

It has been a week since my first trial. My ribs are broken, but luckily they did not break my leg. I can put weight on it, but I still have shooting pain when I walk.

Slowly stepping out of the shower, I wrap a towel around my waist. I hear my phone beep from inside my bedroom. Walking with a limp, I pick up my phone, seeing an unknown number on the screen.

Looking at the clock on my nightstand, it's already 4 p.m. I have three hours to mentally prepare myself for what is to come. Of course, there is another trial when my body feels like shit and I have a limp. I know they're going to observe how I carry myself after the beating and pinpoint my weakness to use against me.

Opening up the drawer to my nightstand, I pull out Ibuprofen and pop three in my mouth. Sitting on my bed,

I wince as I lie down to get a quick nap in, to gain some strength for tonight. I'll need all the help I can get.

I arrive at a packed warehouse, finding a spot near the back of the lot. What the fuck is going on here? What are they up to? As I approach the front entrance, I observe a small crowd of men and women huddled, smoking cigarettes. They look over at me and nod their heads. Turning toward the door, I yank it open, and I'm confronted with loud cheering. The smell of blood and dirt invade my nose. I squeeze through the crowd, scanning to find the area where I'm supposed to go.

Before I make it to the front of the crowd, a hand is on my shoulder. I spin around to see a masked Wolf behind me. He gestures for me to follow him. As he turns his back, the crowd parts to the side, creating a path. I make my way in his direction, focusing on controlling my limp, hoping they don't notice. He stops abruptly, standing side by side with the two other Wolves.

"Your trial is to fight in the ring of death. Your opponent is a wolf who failed their assignment and was placed on punishment. If they live, they get to stay with the pack. If you live, you get to move on. If I were you, Kingsley, I would try not to die." He gestures me toward the entrance of the ring.

I make my way to the center of the ring as people crowd the sides, watching excitedly to see who my opponent will be. The center of the ring is covered with nothing but dirt and stains of dried blood.

I scan the crowd, catching the eye of Cade. I wonder if he is here for a fight tonight as well.

The crowd goes silent as a six-foot-seven behemoth steps into the ring. He is built like a boulder. Jesus, fuck. You have to be kidding me. He's a good three inches taller and his chest is wider, leaner than me. Observing more of his features, he has a shaved head, with a beard covering his face. He looks me up and down, throwing his head back, laughing, assuming he can take me in a matter of seconds.

A bell chimes, indicating the start of the fight. We circle each other, observing each other's movements and how we carry ourselves. He comes charging at me, swinging, and I duck, avoiding his fist. With the power he put into that swing, he would have knocked me out. I swing my fist to the side, connecting with his ribs. He doesn't even budge. He steps back, lifting his leg and kicking me in the chest. The impact was so hard, my body lifted off the ground flying across the ring, hitting the ground.

I grunt, the wind knocked out of me. Hearing loud stomping coming near, I roll to my side, lifting myself up, but he knees me in the face. I stagger as blood sprays out of my mouth. Turning his back to me, he puts his hands up in the air, causing the crowd to go wild. I rush to my feet, moaning from the pain shooting through my body.

I clench my jaw and rush at him, knocking him off balance. My fist connects with his face, causing a tooth to fly out of his mouth. This fucker just laughs. He gets to his feet, swings, hitting me in my ribs. I bend over, clenching my side. He takes the opportunity to uppercut my jaw. His fists are like the Hulks. How the fuck am I going to win against this man?

I look up to see that he has pulled a switchblade from the back of his jeans and flipped it open.

"Your pretty little face isn't going to be so pretty once I'm done with it." He swings the knife, and I block with my arm before it hits my face.

He gets me in the forearm with a deep gash. I kick his kneecap, and he hits the ground. Ahh, there's your weakness. Scrambling to my feet, I kick at his other kneecap, causing him to wince in pain. I then connect my foot with his face, his head snapping to the left. He then turns his head back in my direction and throws the knife directly into my side.

FUCK. I stagger back with my hand on the handle of the blade. Pulling out the knife, dropping it to the ground as blood leaks out of my wound. Rough hands wrapped around my throat as I'm lifted off the ground. My airways are being cut, causing my hands to fly to my neck, attempting to pry his fingers off. I'm slammed onto my back with this fucker hovering over me, both hands now wrapping around on my neck.

From the corner of my eye, I see shining metal to my left. I reach over, grabbing a fist full of dirt and shove it into his eyes. He lets go of me. Using the opportunity, I reach over, grab the knife, and plunge it into the side of his neck. I hear a gurgle, and blood leaks out of his mouth, spraying all over my face as he fights for air and his bulky body tumbles on top of me.

The crowd goes wild, cheering my name. *Kingsley... Kingsley... Kingsley...* The bell chimes, indicating the fight is over. Two Wolves stand over us, lifting the giant's body off of me. My vision begins to fade as I hear voices above my head.

"He still has a pulse. Get him transported to the infirmary at the church. Notify Dr. Kauffman to meet us there, ready to stitch up this wound." Those are the last words I hear before darkness takes over.

I wake up to bright lights above my head, making me squint. The smell of bleach fills my nose. I sit up, gasping at the pain in my side. Looking around, I'm in some sort of infirmary. The Wolves won't use a hospital during the trials. It would raise too many questions, too many prying eyes. I push myself up, looking down to see a bandage wrapped around my torso and wires hooked up, monitoring my heart.

"You took one hell of a beating. Good to see you didn't die." My father strides into the room. He hands me a bottle of water, and I unscrew the cap, taking a deep swig.

"You must be proud, seeing your son all fucked up. Were you there?" I ask, giving him the side eye, as I lie back down on the bed.

"Yes. I'm surprised to see you were able to complete the trial, considering that was one of our best men," he says, walking over to a clipboard hanging on the wall, picking it up, and reading whatever contents are on it. "You will be fine. Nothing serious is broken and your organs are still intact."

I roll my eyes. "If he was one of our best men, then why was he in the fighting ring?"

"He got too cocky and failed an assignment. Get some rest." He walks out of the room as the door slams behind him.

It's been a couple of weeks since I have heard from Cole and Cade. I've reached out, but no answer from either of them. I wonder if they had their trials and if they survived.

Chapter 3

LOYALTY

Seth

It's been two months since our last task. We made it out pretty fucked up, but we passed. We haven't heard anything from the pack, but I guess they want to see us squirm with anxiety, wondering what and when our next trial will be.

Walking out of the weight room, I head into the locker room to take a quick shower. Sweat, drenching my shirt from the two-hour workout, clings against my body. I'm sure my stench can be detected from a mile away. The locker room is empty, which is a win for me. There's a guy that's normally here at this time that always stops me in my tracks and talks to me like we're old friends. He's lonely, but I'm not in the mood to sit here for two hours as he goes off about the events that occurred during the week. Finding my locker, twisting the knob, and entering my code, I hear a click and the door opens. I lift my shirt over my head and drop my pants to the floor, along with my boxers. Grabbing my toiletries and a towel, I shove my clothes into the locker and head over to another room where the showers are located.

I hit the weights every day and run five miles to keep up my endurance for what is to come. As if that isn't enough, I meet with Cole and Cade to get sparring in at night.

As I reach the showers, I pull the curtain to the side and turn the temperature up as hot as it can go, steaming up the stall. I sit under the raining water and bow my head. The sizzling heat melts the pain and soreness away, rendering me numb. To survive this brutal world, you need to shut it all off.

Lost in my pit of emptiness, the curtain pushes to the side as a figure walks in, closing it behind them. I look up. Morgan...

She has a towel wrapped around her body, which drops to the ground, exposing her naked body. She saunters into the shower stall while swaying her hips, trying to be sexy. Pulling the curtains shut, she eye-fucks me as she observes my body, licking her lips.

"What are you doing here?" I ask. Morgan is my ex, who I initially used to get under Regan's skin, and it worked. Each time she had seen us together, her eyes blazed with hatred. Morgan ended up being around longer than intended, like a leech, but she was a good fuck.

I eventually caught her sucking off some random punk at a party. Regardless of the fact that I used her to make my little spawn jealous, she was mine to have until I was done. Those who knew me knew better than to touch what was mine. I saw red, grabbed her by the hair, and threw her across the floor away from him. I had stalked my prey, clenching my fists, and beat the shit out of the guy.

I can't stand the sight of her, but she has a nice pussy when I need to relieve myself. I know she'll pick up when I call. She's always been a good little slut.

"I've been watching you, Seth. Just when I thought you couldn't get any hotter, you keep me on my toes. Yet, you haven't reached out in a long time. It's a little concerning since the last time we were together, we had a good fuck. Don't you miss how good I make you feel?" She looks at me with those slutty, seductive eyes, grabbing my thick cock in her small hands. She strokes me hard and fast as her lips touch my neck, kissing and sucking. I'm hard instantly.

I can't lie, she's fucking attractive. The need to bury my cock deep inside of her is growing by the minute, just one more time. I can't keep this going with her, especially once I become a Wolf. I can't have the conniving, untrustworthy slut around the others. How many other beds will she jump into?

I slam her against the shower wall and wrap my hand around her neck, squeezing to cut off all but a sliver of her airway. She sucks in a breath as I wrap her leg around my hip, slamming my cock inside of her. I pound into her as she cries, panting with pleasure. Her hands are clawing at her neck, trying to remove my hand. I thrust harder, deeper, and faster inside of her. Her throat works under my hand as she tries to scream as she hits her climax. I pull out of her before I cum, throwing her to the ground.

"You got what you wanted. Now get out of my sight for good. Stay out of my way." I pin my eyes on her, challenging her to argue with me.

"Seth, what the fuck? I'm good for you to fuck, but you throw me away as soon as you're done? Everything that happened in the past, I've learned and am trying to redeem myself. I thought you would take me as your ol' lady." She looks at me with tears in her eyes. Fake tears, if you ask me.

"Morgan, we both know you tried climbing in Cade's bed the other night. Want me to go on with the list of Wolves you seek out? You're a good fuck, but I'm done. This is completely done." I shut the shower off, walking around her and leaving her on the ground as she curses and screams. I head out the door, entering the locker room to get dressed. As I'm pulling on my pants, I hear a ding. Picking my phone up from the locker, I open my phone.

I grab my bag, place my gun in my back waistband, and head out of the gym. I climb into the truck, starting up the engine, and head to the old church. As I pull up, I see Cole and Cade stepping out of their own vehicles. As I walk up, I notice another figure walking toward us. I nod at the boys, and we all reach behind our belts, raising our guns to point at this figure.

"Isn't this church creepy as hell? I don't know why they don't just burn this shit down," the guy says as he walks up to us. He has sandy blonde hair, is about six-foot, and is dressed in all black. As he approaches, he has a smirk on his face, looking us up and down.

"Who the fuck are you? And why are you here? Last time I checked, I didn't see you as part of the trials. In fact, I have never seen you around town." Cole looks at him with daggers, gripping his gun tighter.

"Well, don't you know how to welcome a new member? My name is Damon. I just had my first trial last night. Lucky for you, you have me with you for your next trial. So, get off my ass and let's get this shit over with." He pushes past Cole, heading toward the church.

Before he can take another step, I grab his arm, throwing him into the side of my truck. The force of the impact causes him to slide to the ground. I lift my gun, shoving the barrel to his temple. "You think we are stupid enough to let you walk into the church, believing a word you say?" I say, digging my barrel harder, which makes him wince.

"You must be Seth. Why don't you call your father? He's an Elder, right? My grandfather was an Elder before he died—Nicholas Stevenson. The Elders won't be too pleased knowing you have a gun to my head." Lowering my gun, I crack my neck as I watch him get to his feet, dusting himself off and striding toward the entrance once again.

Something about him doesn't sit right with me, but I can't touch him yet. After this trial is completed, I will be paying my father a visit to confirm what we were told. For now, we don't have time. You don't make the Wolves wait.

As we enter the old church, the floorboards creak with every step we take. The room is dimly lit by candles scattered throughout the open area. Looking straight ahead, three men stand with their arms crossed in front of their chests, dressed in red hoodies with the wolf masks shielding their identities. Now that I'm standing in front of them, not drugged and beaten to a pulp, I take in the masks. They are gunmetal gray, with gear sockets above the right eyebrows and sides. There are tubes on the right side that connect from the snout up behind the ears. The detail of the indents of the masks gives the illusion of fur.

A fourth Wolf steps between the three, wearing an all-black hoodie and a wolf mask with red eyes piercing through. This must be an Elder joining in tonight, delivering our trial details. Everyone has the same disguise, unless they are an elder. With him being here, this means we absolutely cannot fuck this up and get ourselves killed.

"You have entered your third trial. This will test your loyalty. A judge has declared separation from the Empire and participated in an unforgivable act. In this act, he was joined by his brothers. None are to be left alive—make it clean. Make it as if they have vanished, with no traces to the Wolves. You're to wear your mask at all times to hide your identity, and hoodies to cover any markings that can be identified. Three days is what you're given to complete this task. Work together and prove your loyalty to not only the Wolves but to each other. The four of you are all you have. Complete this trial, and you will move forward to the last and final stage."

"How many brothers are there?" I tilt my head with an evil smirk, already feeling the excitement running through me. I live for this; I am Satan.

"There are three brothers and the judge. In this envelope are recent locations where they have been spotted, photos of their identities, and a USB with a video we have discovered. Once you complete the trial, bring us a thumb from each of them, as well as the rings they wear." With that, the Wolves turn and exit the building.

Taking the envelope, we pile into our vehicles and meet back at my house.

Spreading out the documents, we study the photos of their faces and a two story home, and learn the judge has sentenced an ex-Wolf to four years of prison and parole instead of death. The Wolves are not happy. Sliding my laptop over and plugging in the USB, a black screen appears. After a few seconds, the feed flashes to a cell with a female hunched over, chained to a chair.

Her face is not visible as her hair is shielding her identity, but the way her dirty body is slumped, one can tell she has been mistreated. Why are we watching this? I don't understand.

Four men walk into the room, circling her like they are getting ready to devour their prey. I am assuming she says something because the judge backhands her, snapping her head to the side. We can't hear what is being said, as there is no audio, but I can assume it was a smart-ass comment.

He then yanks her head back by her hair, revealing her face. My heart stops. She spits, cackling, as he wipes the spit from his face. He pulls out a pocket knife, flipping out the blade and plunges the knife into her stomach. Pulling it out, the act is repeated twenty more times. I count.

My body starts to vibrate with rage. The glass cup I have in my hand cracks and shatters from gripping it so hard. The glass penetrates deep into my hand, but I don't care.

"Jesus, fuck. Bailey," Cade whispers.

"Seth, turn this off. You don't need to watch this." Cole reaches over to click the pause button, moving the cursor to exit out, but stops as I grab hold of his wrist.

"Don't fucking touch the computer. I need to see this. I need to know how they did it." The walls around me feel like they are closing in around me—suffocating. But I need to see this. I need to know how to make them feel what she felt. So, I click play.

Unchaining Bailey from the chair, her body crashes to the floor. She isn't moving. She isn't getting up. He unzips his pants as he hovers over her body. One of the brothers walks over to her and rips off her pants, positioning her ass in the air. The judge gets on his knees and whips out his dick, slamming it into her ass. He holds onto her hips as he thrusts into her over and over again. Once he finishes and pulls out, blood seeps from where he fucked her.

Each brother takes their turn with her, fucking her lifeless body. Blood pools underneath her from the stab wounds. How do you find pleasure fucking a dead body? Sick fucks. After they finish with her, a brother looks up, finds a pipe, and throws a chain around it to hang her body by her neck. Cutting her shirt open, they expose her completely. Pulling out their phones, they take photos of her hanging naked, dead. They admire their work like it's the best fucking art piece ever made, swinging side to side in front of them.

After they get their fill and entertainment, the judge walks out of the frame and the brothers take her down, cutting off her head and carrying it outside the frame. The feed cuts off, going back to a black screen.

Running to the trash can, I empty my stomach. When I have nothing else, I continue to dry heave. My humanity starts to slip. My sister didn't deserve this.

I black out, and glass goes flying across the kitchen. Barstools are destroyed from being smashed against the island. I feel arms wrap around me, pushing my body to the ground, pinning me.

"Calm down, Seth. You will deliver his fate. But you need to calm down and think clearly." It takes both boys to pin me down on the floor to keep me from destroying anything else. Damon stays off to the side as he observes what is transpiring.

If I have anything to do with it, Hell won't even let these fuckers in.

I didn't sleep. I couldn't, with the images of Bailey clouding my brain.

The next day, we quickly gather our supplies, shoving everything in our bags and yanking our black hoodies on.

Placing full-face masks over our faces, we complete the disguise by pulling the hoods over our heads. Silencers are placed on our pistols, tucking them into the back of our pants.

We sit in silence for several hours as we head to this home. No one speaks. Everyone stares at their phones the whole ride without a sound. Me? I stare straight ahead, shutting my mind off, becoming numb and lethal.

Pulling into the woods near the target location, but keeping a safe distance so we do not get noticed, I kill the engine. The last thing we need is for our truck to be seen and for the brothers to suspect us. One by one, filing out of the truck, we make sure we have everything we need. Each of us picks a tree in the woods on the outskirts of the property. We climb up into the branches to keep us hidden, while also giving us a better view of the property and house.

A man walks out the front door, speaking into his phone. He looks like he is arguing with someone, based on his demeanor and body language. He paces back and forth along the gravel of the driveway.

I glance at the boys and nod, signaling them to jump down and advance, but I freeze when I see a little girl walk out the front door, running over to the man.

"Daddy, Daddy. It is supper time. Mama says to come inside," I hear the little girl say in her high pitch squeals. My guess is no older than six years old. I hold my fist up again. We may be monsters, but we don't harm children. The noises fade as they head into the two-story house.

"I knew that would have been too easy. How the hell are we going to eliminate him with children in the house?" Cade growls. "WE DO NOT HARM CHILDREN."

"We will sit and watch the house and figure out a plan without being seen or heard. Now, do us all a favor and shut the fuck up before we are heard," I growl back.

The sky begins to darken, and we have been scoping out the property for the last couple of hours. Suddenly, a woman comes out of the house and the children run past her toward the vehicle.

"Let me know once you get to your sister's safely. I will call you in the morning. I love you," I hear him say to the female, who I am assuming is his wife. He gives her a quick kiss before she gets into her car and drives off.

A black SUV enters the driveway shortly after the woman and children leave. Three men get out of the vehicle, approaching the judge. They clasp each other's hands, heading back into the house.

That was our signal. The issue was eliminated before we even came up with a plan to avoid the innocent bystanders in the house.

"Cole and Damon, you two stick together. Go through the back and see if you can get into the house. Cade, you will come with me. We will go up to the balcony. Be quiet and don't be seen." I head toward the house to climb the wall.

Once we get up the wall and onto the balcony, I peek in to see if anyone is moving around and jiggle the handle. Cade comes up right behind me, scanning the area. I work the door, picking the lock. I hear a click and open the door. We slowly slide into the empty room, looking around the elegant decor in what looks like a master suite.

Hearing footsteps from the hall, Cade slips behind a curtain as I slip behind the bathroom door. The judge walks into the room, directly to a dresser, and rummages through a drawer. He has his back to me. I come out behind the door, taking silent steps behind him.

As he turns around, he jumps back, and I cock my head to the side, raising my hand and waving my fingers. "Who the fuck are you?"

Before he can say more, I slam my fist into the side of his face. He topples over, hitting a nightstand. I pounce on him, fist flying as I pound in his face over and over again. As I raise my fist, I scream in his face, "Why did you do it?" I repeat my question over and over again as his stupid ass face scrunches in confusion. "Why did you kill Bailey?" My body vibrates. I can feel my control slipping.

His face goes pale, shaking his head. "I can explain. Please, please don't kill me. I have kids," he cries.

"Oh, I'm going to kill you. And I am going to kill you the same way you killed Bailey." I tip my head back, cackling.

"Cade, break the chair leg and hand it to me." He does, walking over and handing it to me. I kick the judge over onto his stomach as he begs, thrashing to get away. Cade must know what is on my mind because he strides over, bending down and holding the man in place. Ripping down his pants, his bare, hairy ass points up toward the ceiling. I don't give a warning and shove the chair leg up his ass. Screams fill the room, like music to my ears.

I pull it out and shove it again and again. Blood trickles down his legs. After I finish the assault, we flip him to his back. His eyes are heavy, but he is still alive.

"The only favor I'm doing for you is saving your children from discovering that the monsters aren't under their bed, but really the very person who is supposed to protect them." Grabbing a knife from my pocket, I flip the blade open and stab him twenty times. The same amount he did with my sister. Blood coats my mask, my jacket, the ground. His body slumps, lifeless.

Cade grabs a plastic bag, and with his gloved hands, cuts the judge's thumb off, putting it in a bag along with his ring he takes off his index finger. The silver bulky ring has a howling wolf on it—what a disgrace.

"It's done. We took care of the brokers—grabbed the rings and the ugly ass thumbs." Cole and Damon walk into the room, pausing, examining the destruction lying on the floor.

After taking care of the bodies and mess, we head back to the truck and pile in. Cole shoots a text to the Elders, indicating the trial has been completed. After a three-hour drive, we pull up to the church. The church looks spooky at night, like it has paranormal beings waiting to be discovered. Grabbing the items needed, we make our way in.

The three red-hooded Wolves stand behind the black-hooded Wolf, waiting for our delivery.

"We see you made it out alive and trust you eliminated the problem." The Elder speaks, addressing me as if I am the leader.

"They have been handled. Bodies and all evidence have been disposed of," I confirm, handing over the baggy full of thumbs and rings.

Before I can say or ask about the USB, the Elder strides out a side door of the church as a red-hooded Wolf collects the bag. They too turn away and head out of the church with not one word or glance. We glance at each other, eyebrows raised, and head back to the truck. Damon disappears without a word, like a ghost not wanting to be seen.

We change, stuffing our dirty hoodies and masks into a bag, and place it in a hidden compartment in the truck. I need to speak with my father about some things, but I can feel the crash coming. I wonder if he has seen the video—if he is the Elder who delivered this to me as punishment.

Chapter 4

SETH

It's been a couple of days since our trial. I slept. My body couldn't be moved as I finally shut down from exhaustion. No dreams appeared as I was in oblivion, with nothing but darkness around me. Maybe that is a good thing. Seeing my sister's murder play over and over in my head when I don't sleep is torture enough.

After I shower, I head out to meet my father to discuss concerns about Damon since he has arrived. No one knew who he was or where he came from. I need answers. I need to confirm he is who he says he is. Something about him rubs me the wrong way. My judgments of character have never failed me.

Walking into my father's office, I find him hunched over, drowning in paperwork. He has dark circles around his eyes, his hair is starting to gray, and his body is screaming at him for rest. "Are you going to continue to stand there staring, or are you going to come in, boy?"

"Did you know? Did you see the video?" I eye him for some sort of emotion.

"Yes. I would rather keep it out of this house to avoid your mother hearing. She does not need to relive her death. I am the reason your trial was to eliminate them. It was your duty to avenge your sister." His eyes stare at me with so much hollowness.

"Now, tell me, to what do I owe the pleasure of your presence today, Seth?" he huffs impatiently.

"Damon. The guy that showed up to our trial. He claims his grandfather is Nicholas Stevenson. Why was he joining us?" Sitting down in the chair in front of his desk, I spread my arms across the back of the chairs.

"Why are you questioning the Elders?" Narrowing his eyes, he looks me up and down.

"Because he has never been seen in this town. We know nothing about him—if he is lying or loyal." My temper starts to spike.

"Need I remind you that just because you are my son, it does not mean I owe you an answer? We are doing our research on this boy. We don't fully trust him, but we want him close. Keep an eye on him, and once you have the privilege of knowing more, we will involve you."

"Your trials are nearing the end. You better hope all the Elders deem you worthy."

"After the trials, I plan on continuing with my club plans as my future with the Wolves. I want to start now, so it is up and running as soon as possible. I have found a location, but it is owned by the Wolves. Can you speak with the others to allow me to lease the warehouse? I have saved up the funds for the renovation, stock, and opening. I have built connections for the traffic to flow in, bringing not only money for myself, but the Wolves," I say, changing the subject, as I don't want to get into how unworthy I am in his eyes.

"I will speak with them, just know we will ask for a price. There is a basement under the club. That is to be used for Wolf business and the torturing of any enemies or traitors. But if you don't pass the trials, you will be dead. And the club will be under our control." I get up from my seat, heading toward the office doors.

Turning around, I notice he is observing me, seeing how I react to the demand—to the dig that there is a possibility I will be dead. "Understood."

Chapter 5

INITIATION

Seth

It has been six months since our last trial. When you're waiting for the next trial or initiation, you never know when you will be called.

I recently bought a warehouse on St. Louis Street and turned it into a thriving night club. Within months of being opened, my club has become the center point of the city, considering we are located in New Orleans, the spot for tourists to come see Mardi Gras, witchcraft, voodoo, and hauntings. My office is above the dance floor, with windows overlooking the club. No one can see through the windows from the outside, but I can watch everything that goes on.

Below the dance floor is a basement chamber, which is to be used for interrogation and beatings. The Wolves bring their prospects in after hours and use my chambers, as it is out of sight and out of mind. The agreement with the Elders is to have my club up and running. Cole and Cade work in my club as bouncers, as well as help with business and torturing for the Wolves.

Per usual, my father is disappointed in my career choice. As the only child left, it was expected that I would take a more influential employment role, giving the Wolves the advantage and preparing me to inherit my father's legacy. I didn't want an elite career as a judge, officer, or even politician. It's just not who I am, and my father is disappointed because now our family won't have another person to control the aspects of the town or what happens. I may not be any of those choices, but I am treated as if I run this town. I have gained respect with the Elders all on my own, regardless of who my father is.

I am proud of my accomplishments, but I could lose it all in a blink of an eye, since I have not been initiated yet. If I do not complete the trials, I will not live. It is as simple as that. There are too many secrets for them to risk keeping me alive. I am not weak; I will move forward.

It's 2 p.m., and I'm sitting in my office going through expenses and orders before the club opens. We have re-models needing to be done for the bar and also for the basement. I need to finish soundproofing the door and the walls for the basement before the Elders need them for use. The last thing we need are eyes on the club for screaming coming from below. My phone vibrates with an incoming message.

Unknown: Come to the back of the club.
You have 5 minutes.

I get up from the chair and head out of the office. I take the stairs down two at a time, and when I get to the bottom, I see Cole and Cade walking toward me.

"Did you guys get the same text?" I nod at the boys.

"Yeah—little late in the game, don't you think? They had to keep us waiting six months?" Cade shakes his head, walking behind me toward the door.

I push it open. Stepping outside, I am surprised to not find anyone waiting. Suddenly, I see a figure at the side of my vision, and then I feel the bat connect with my ribs. I clench my teeth and bring my hands to my ribs, sucking in a breath.

I hear a clank, and then chains wrap around my neck. My hands grasp the chains, trying to pull them free, but a bag is placed over my head. They drag me about ten feet and toss me into the back of a van. I feel two thuds next to me, which I can only assume are Cole and Cade. The door slams shut, and the van's tires squeal as the van jerks into motion. About fifteen minutes later, the van comes to a stop. I hear both the driver and the passenger side doors close and the crunching of rocks as they make their way to the back. The doors fly open and we are yanked out and thrown to the ground.

They drag us up a dirt driveway and throw us onto a concrete floor on our knees. The bags are yanked off our heads, and I quickly take in my surroundings. In front of me is a stone wolf fountain altar with a red substance at the base. Looking to the side, I see melted candles, providing dim lighting. Turning my head, I notice we are back in the old church. Three red-hooded Wolves appear, holding the wolf masks and hoodies. The black-hooded Wolf strides behind with a knife in their hand. As they stop in front of us, one of them reaches down, taking the chains off our necks and motioning for us to rise.

"You have made it through the trials. You have proven your loyalty and ability to complete what is asked of you in a timely, clean manner. Tonight, you join the Empire of Wolves. Once you're initiated into the Empire, you are in for life and can never escape. Seth, come forward and make your oath." The black-hooded, masked Wolf turns toward me.

I step forward. I have been trained my whole life for this moment.

"I, Seth Kingsley, take an oath with my loyalty to the brotherhood and the Empire of Wolves. I am to serve and protect the Wolves with my life." After I make my oath, I howl, filling the silent church. I'm handed a knife and advised to make an offering to the fountain to show respect and binding. Slitting my wrist, not deep, but enough for blood to form. I walk over, looking up at the wolf structure with pride. Hovering my wrist above, I let a few drops of blood drip into the chamber pools.

A red-hooded Wolf walks forward with a metal wolf mask and places it on my face. I am handed a red hoodie. Placing the red hoodie above my head, I slide it down my body. Cole and Cade take their oath and present their offering. I look to the left and see tables set up with machines I didn't notice before. Other Wolves walk out, taking their places at the tables, setting up their machines. A few others come out with chairs, bringing them to the assigned spots.

"Being part of the pack, you will now be marked with a tattoo of a wolf on your chest. Step up to the tables and complete the final initiation."

I step up to the table and sit on the chair provided. Pulling the hood above my head, I place it on the chair. As I sit, getting comfortable, the chair reclines back. My eyes travel to the ceiling as they rub ointment across my chest. They place a stencil, making sure it is aligned and smoothed before transferring it to my chest. Slowly, they peel the paper back and start up the tattoo machine. Buzzing fills my ears as the needles penetrate my skin.

That's it. We are now part of the pack, and there is no going back.

Welcome to the Empire of Wolves. This is where hell begins...

Chapter 6

PRESENT

Regan

It has been four years since I have been home. I had left New Orleans and went to college at the University of Alabama. I had to get out of this shithole. Everyone loves New Orleans with the witches, voodoo, and Mardi Gras, but it is not all about that. When you grow up with a father who is an Elder for the Empire of Wolves, you are constantly exposed to violence. But here I am, coming back home. Once you live here, you always come back.

I pull up in my Silverado to my family's home, life growing from the flower boxes and flower pots and a fountain in the center of the driveway. The house is a Victorian mansion that is painted black with dark midnight shutters and vines running up the foundation of the home. I put my truck in park, grab my bag, and step out of the truck. I head up the steps and the door swings open as my father and mother step out. My little brother runs past them, nearly knocking me down with a hug.

"About time you returned home. If you would have just gone to college closer, we could have gotten a head start on your future, but as it is, we have a lot to discuss." My father pins me with a stern look. I haven't walked through the door yet before he starts on his lectures.

"Dear, what your father means is we missed you. We're glad that you're home safe." My mother gives me a warm smile with her blushed face. My mother is a warm, kind, caring woman. How she married my father is beyond me. She deserves better than a man who sees her as a play toy and a doormat.

"Dad, I want to pursue my own dreams, my own life outside of this shithole. I had to get out and experience life on my own." Plus, I don't take orders from anyone. I've always been the disobedient, wild card of a child. Never playing by rules. Sure as hell wasn't going to be stuck here, like my mother, but I don't say this to him.

"Then why are you back? If you can make your own choices and want out of this 'shithole', then turn back around," he huffs as he narrows his eyes at me.

"You know why I'm back. Things didn't work out. I'm not getting into this with you." Pushing past my parents, walking up the stairs toward my room. Opening the doors, I throw my bag on the floor, and flop down on my bed. I need a drink—or five. He's starting shit already and I haven't even been here for five minutes. Maybe this was a bad decision. I pull out my phone, looking for my best friend's contact and send a text.

Me: Please tell me you're not busy and want to meet for drinks?

Alex: Bitch, you know I am always down for drinks. Meet me at the Serpent on St Louis.

Me: New club?

Alex: I keep forgetting you left before it opened. It has amazing drinks and yummy men ;)

Me: Sounds promising; be there in 30 min.

I put my phone down on my bed, heading into the bathroom and turning on the shower. Stripping down completely naked, I step into the steaming water. Washing the earlier bullshit off, I feel my muscles relax from the blazing water streaming down my body. Turning off the faucet, I step out, wrapping a fluffy white towel over myself, and head to my gigantic walk-in closet. I grab a brown tight dress that hugs my curves in all the right places. The dress hits above the knees, showing just enough cleavage to leave some imagination to onlookers. I grab my black Vans and head out of the closet. I touch up my makeup, blow dry my hair, and get dressed. My black leather jacket is thrown on top, spraying on Halle Berry perfume. Looking at myself in the mirror, I smile, fully satisfied with my look.

I tiptoe down the stairs, slip through the front door without being heard and jump into the driver's seat of my truck to drive off before my father notices me leaving. The last thing I need is the third degree down my back.

About five minutes later, I turn onto St. Louis Street, parking my truck along the curb. I get out and stare up at the building. It's 4 p.m. and it already has people coming in and out. I wonder who owns this club. As I walk through the doors, it is dim lit, with nice red velvet couches in one corner with an antique coffee table in the center—must be the VIP area. There are high tops surrounding the giant dance floor, and black and red velvet curtains hanging at the windows.

"Regan, over here! You look HOT!" screams Alexandra from across the bar. Oh, how I missed my loudmouth best friend. "You rebel, I don't remember you having those tattoos and nose ring! Time away really has done you justice!" What she doesn't know is that it has been quite the opposite.

"Hi to you, Alex. It is really nice to have someone who is actually excited to see me and not pressuring me to work for their business. I really do need to get a job, but not with him." I roll my eyes, leaning in next to her at the bar.

"That bad of a homecoming, huh? Your dad has a real knack for showing his love," she says, placing a hand over her heart.

"Enough about my dad. He already gives me a headache. How are you doing? What have I missed? I want all the details." I smile at her and nudge her on the shoulder.

"Well, for starters, I work here, bartending. Pays well, and honestly, it is a blast. I might be dating Cole..." As those words leave her mouth, I spit my drink all over the bar.

"When the hell did that start? Alex, he's in line for the Wolves. Do you really want to get tangled up with all that bullshit?" I shake my head, grabbing a napkin.

"Regan, you can relax. We have been seeing each other for a few months. He is already a Wolf, and it's all fun right now. We aren't married." She throws her head back, laughing.

"Hey, Alex, I know you're off, but I'm in need of a bartender. It's about to get really busy with Mardi Gras coming up, and I am short-handed. Do any of you know someone interested?" the tall, dark haired, handsome bartender asks.

"Actually, I do. I was bartending while I was away at college. I happen to need a job. Where can I apply?" I smile big, giving a flirty look. He turns his head over to me, looking me up and down. "My name is Regan, by the way."

"Great, you start tonight as a trial run. If you do well, we will talk about bringing you on permanently."

I hear a door shut behind me, heavy footsteps clouding my ears. As I look over my shoulder, I see three figures in suits walking past. Holy shit, is that Seth Kingsley? This cocky, selfish asshole was attractive then, but now, I can bet his ego has skyrocketed. If Hell was on fire, he would be one alluring Satan. Even in the blackout suit, I can see the muscles bulging out from his chest and arms. His hands and neck are full of tattoos, dark hair, sharp jaw, six-foot-four of—what the hell am I thinking? He looks over at me, sneering like I am a speck of dirt on the floor.

I push off the bar, rolling my eyes. "Catch you later, Alex. I need to run." Looking back over at the bartender.

"Eight p.m. is the time to be here tonight, if that is what you were going to ask," the bartender informs me without looking up from cleaning the glass in his hand.

"Got it. See you tonight." I walk past the three figures, hurrying right out the door.

My heart is racing a mile a minute, breaking a sweat at the back of my neck. What is wrong with me? Last time I saw Seth, he wanted nothing to do with me. He made that fucking clear. I shake my head. Don't be dumb, Regan. You're a strong ass woman who doesn't look back, no matter how mouthwatering he has became.

I was so caught up in my thoughts that I walked right into a figure, whose hot coffee spills down the front of my dress. Fuck, that's burns. Looking up, I lock eyes with a six-foot, muscular, blonde god. Where are all these sexy men coming from? "I am so sorry!" I say, my face reddening from embarrassment.

As he smiles, a dimple on his left cheek appears. "Don't worry about it. I wasn't paying attention, either. What is your name? I haven't seen you around. Damon." He stretches his hand out to me.

"Regan. I just came home from college. It's been years." I blush as he eyes me up and down. "Can I buy you another coffee?"

"I would rather you give me your number, and we can meet for dinner. To replace the coffee, I mean." Smooth dude, real smooth!

"I don't know you. You expect me to hand over my number?" Crossing my arms over my chest, I observe his body language.

"Well, you did run into me. You also said it's been years since being back here. Maybe you can use a new friend?" His eyebrows raise into an arch. "One dinner. If it happens to be the worst time of your life, you can delete and block my number."

"Fine, one dinner, but I really have to go." We exchange numbers, departing in opposite directions.

I'll go out with him one time to make up for the mess I caused, but after that, I need to focus on myself. I need to heal.

Heading back home, I take a deep breath. Tonight will be the night that I change my future and start over.

Chapter 7

SETH

I walk into my office, sitting down at my desk. She's back. My little spawn is back. She definitely came into herself. I almost didn't recognize her—her red hair, nose piercings, tattoos decorating her arm, big chest, and juicy ass. My dick twitches in my jeans at just the thought of my hands grabbing that ass and breathing in her scent.

I know she saw me, knowing who I was as she took off out of the bar. Maybe I shouldn't have given her the disgusted look; she is anything but that. However, I didn't want her to see my excitement at her being home. Another part of me is wondering why she is here. I thought she would be able to get out of the Wolves' grasp and start a new life.

Throughout the years, I've caught myself thinking about her. Is she safe? Is she happy? Letting her go was one of the hardest things I've ever done. But what happened to my sister—I could not let that happen to her. My sister's words echoed in my mind. *"She is good, better than all of us,"* reminding me it had to be done.

"Damn, did you see her? I am pretty sure that was Regan. I didn't know she was coming back, and she is hot." Cade smirks, looking out the office window. "Should have kept her when you had her wrapped around your finger, Seth, 'cause now, the Wolves are going to devour her."

"No one touches, looks at, or gets near her. Anyone who tries, I want to know. I want them brought to me. She is mine. I will destroy anyone who touches her." I raise my eyes at Cade, blazing daggers at him. Where the hell did that come from? I took one look at her and went feral. She isn't even mine.

"Damn, I just thought she was free game since you gave her up years ago. But now she's back, looking like that. You didn't show interest at all down there. Didn't even speak a word." He puts his hands up, shakes his head, and walks out the door.

Cole is lounging on the couch, head back, with his eyes closed. "So, what you're saying is, you won't take her as yours, but you don't want anyone else to have her? Look, man, you either get over this bullshit thought process and give in, or you let her be."

"You, of all people, know exactly why I gave her up years ago. I thought she ran off and was going to stay away. Maybe I fucked up, but I was trying to protect her from our world—from the drugs, the killings, and the Wolves. If the Snakes knew I had someone I valued, they would use her against me. I couldn't do that to her, but she's back." I sigh. I never open up to anyone except Cole, no offense to Cade. Cole has just been through some shit growing up, and we didn't always let Cade in back then.

We have had issues with the Snakes. There is a war pending at any time.

I pull out my phone and dial down to the bar. "Chris, what was said when you spoke with Regan Dale earlier today?" I peer down out the window to the bar floor, observing.

"The redhead? Wait, that's Regan Dale? I needed a bartender; she wanted a job. She starts tonight at eight for a trial run. I figured you wouldn't care, as long as we got another helping hand."

"Hire her permanently. When she starts, make sure you keep an eye on her, and let me know if anyone touches her or gives her any shit. Have her working at your bar. You will split the sections during her shift." I hang up my phone and lean back in my chair.

With her working for me, I can keep a closer eye on her—learn her triggers, what pisses her off, and see whom she associates with. There has to be a reason she is back.

She swore off this town, left so quickly, without batting an eye. Maybe her father brought her home. I wonder if she still has that sass that always drove me crazy, giving me a run for my money. I always liked a challenge.

That little spawn will be mine. And I will be Satan, who ruins her. I'll make her beg for me to give her mercy.

Chapter 8

Regan

Seeing Seth made my blood boil, but also triggered feelings and thoughts that made me clench my legs. He is so fucking handsome with those pining eyes, making me want to crawl on the ground for him and beg him to take me. I shake my head. I can't think like that. Getting mixed up with him is dangerous. Everything I had worked hard to get away from would be ruined.

I walk into my room, throwing my bag on the bed, and head to the shower to get this coffee smell off of me. I undress and step under the streaming water. Closing my eyes, I let the sultry water stream down my body. My mind wanders to Seth—to the way he was looking at me with those sneering eyes.

My mind drifts to a place I know I should not even go, but my hand travels down to my body. I imagine what his body looks like under that tight suit: bulging muscles, tight chest, and thick, strong hands. Just the thought of his hands caressing my tits makes my body tingle. As my hand stops at my vagina, my fingers create circles over my clit. A moan escapes me as I envision his hands traveling to my neck, wrapping his thick fingers around my throat. I plunge my fingers into my cunt, pumping my fingers in and out.

Bending me over, ripping my thong off with a snap, he spreads my legs as he shoves his hard, thick cock inside of me. He thrusts back and forth, causing slapping noises to fill the room from our entangled bodies. Lifting my leg to the side of the tub, I pump my two fingers harder as I tilt my head back. A moan escapes my throat along with ragged breaths filling the bathroom. Images of his body pressed against mine, as our bodies are entwined as one, flash in my mind as I shove my fingers deeper inside, hitting my G-spot like a bullseye. My thumb massaging my clitoris puts me over the edge, cumming all over my fingers. I take deep, shaky breaths as I quickly wash off my body and hair and shut the shower off. Grabbing a towel to wrap around my naked body, I step out, sitting on the lid of the toilet. I can't believe I got myself off thinking about Seth—wanting him to fill me with his manhood and devour me. What is wrong with me?

After I get ready, I head to the club for my first shift. My father was not happy to find out that I got a job at a club instead of working for him, but I need to show that I am independent. I don't need to rely on him or the Wolves.

I walk in, approaching my new boss, Chris. He gives me a rundown on the specials, where everything is, and starts setting up for the night. Since I have experience bartending, I don't need training. The night starts, and the crowd comes in fast. The DJ is blasting music and strobe lights fill the club. It's going to be a great night.

Throughout the night, Chris and I split the bar in two. He is on one side, and I am on the other, juggling the endless crowd. I am glad we are stationed together, as I am still learning some of the specialty drinks, like the Witch's Brew, Voodoo Doll, and the Boiling Cauldron. They are all fruity drinks, but nothing like the Long Island Iced Tea, Sex on the Beach, or Adios drinks I was used to making.

Females dance on the bar without a care in the world! A couple of girls want to take body shots from my tits. Chris didn't care, as long as it was not a male. I guess they protect their females from prying hands.

The men pay me to thrust water onto their faces, following with a cringing smack. They get two shots for that. They had to sign a waiver beforehand, advising they would not retaliate or touch the female bartenders. Why would someone want to be wet with a throbbing cheek? No idea, but they tip well, so I'm not complaining.

It is about 1 a.m. and the energy of the club is amazing, full of laughs, smiles, and flirting. I move along the bar, getting drinks, and feeling alive. I walk up to a group of guys.

"Hey there, gorgeous, you must be new here." A guy with brown shaggy hair, wearing a black tee speaks to me first.

"What can I get ya?" I shoot him a flirtatious smile, leaning over the bar top.

"Get me a shot of whiskey and maybe some of that ass." He smirks, eyeing me up and down.

"I'll get you a shot." I turned around to grab a glass. This guy had the nerve to reach over the bar and smack my ass. "What the fuck do you think you're doing? Do not touch me. I'll get your drink, but do not touch me, or so help me, God, I will snap your fingers and have you running off, crying for your mommy." I stare at him with fire in my eyes.

"Oh, feisty, I like that. I said I want a shot and some of that ass. It's what I pay for." He grabs me by the arm. My heart starts to race, causing my adrenaline to kick in.

All of a sudden, Seth appears, grabbing the guy's arm and throwing him across the room.

"You do not touch what is mine. You will wish you were dead if you lay a finger on her again," he growls, with fury in his eyes.

I stand there in shock. Did he just say that I was his? I must be hearing things because he has me fucked up if he truly believes that. The guy is shooting daggers at me, blood spilling out of his nose from hitting a table. He gets up off the ground, grabs his jacket off the chair, and darts out of the bar.

"I am not yours, Seth. I am not an object you own. So, why don't you take the smart route and leave the bar like that idiot?" I am shaking at this point. It's not that I am not thankful he got rid of that guy, but that he stuck a claim to me. I am not his.

"Oh, my little spawn. Considering I own this club, you, my dear, work for me. I own you. Now, be a good little spawn and grab me a whiskey."

I stand there with my mouth hanging open. Fuck, he owns this club? How did Alex fail to mention this to me when I spoke up advising that I want the position? If I knew, I would not have said a word. That explains why he was here earlier this afternoon, striding around the club, radiating confidence and power. It's not like I can just quit on the spot like I want to. I just started this job. If I don't want to work for my father, I have to figure something out. I don't want to depend on my parents. My father will just use it against me. I'm trying to get the hell out of the house as it is. Shaking my head, I pour Seth his whiskey, set it in front of him, and shoot him a glare. I head over to the other side of the bar to serve other customers, but mainly to avoid him altogether.

I can feel his eyes on me, burning holes in the side of my head. Why is he watching me? Any other girl would drop dead, rolling around in their grave, if they had Seth Kingsley staring at them, showing them attention and kicking a guy's ass with one throw. Me? Nope. I'm not like other girls. All he is trying to prove is that I am under his control. That I am his. He makes me want to run out of this town again. I don't need another situation like HIM. I want to stab him, but also, the thought of him makes my legs clench. My vagina wants him to show me more of his dominance and games.

This bitch needs to get her act together and stop betraying me.

Chapter 9

SETH

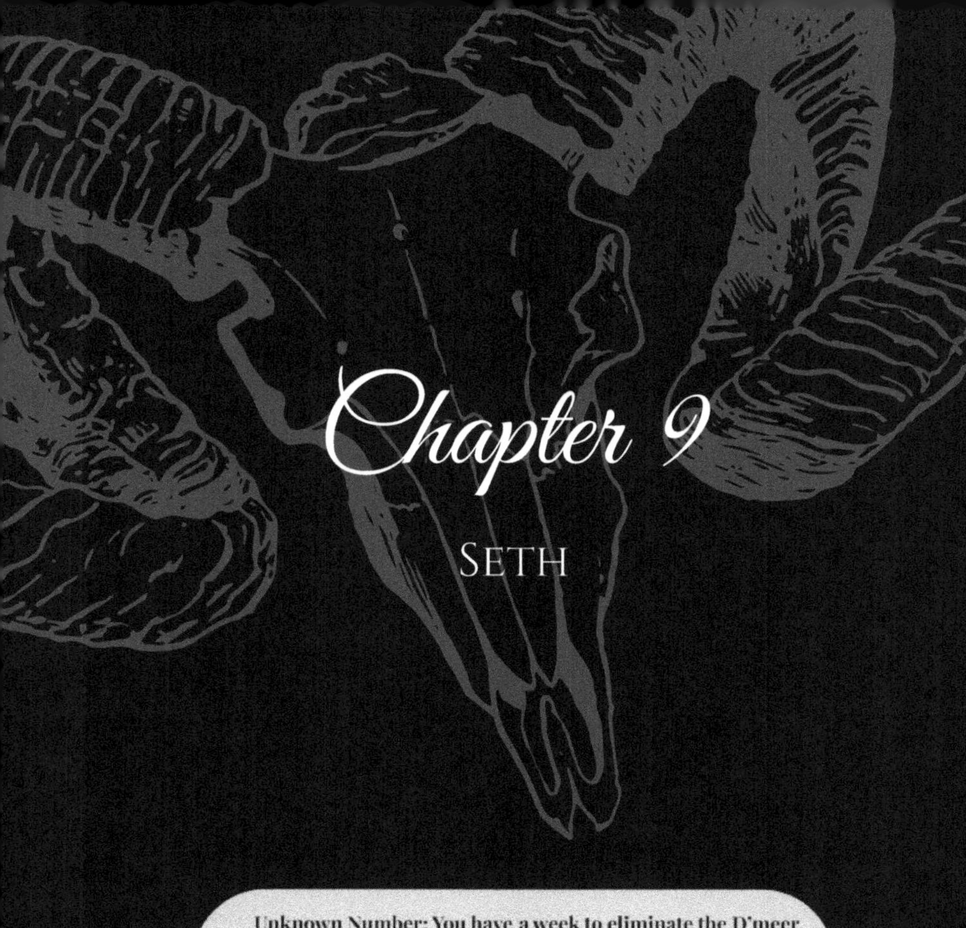

I head over to the church. As I pull up, I see Cole and Cade have been summoned for this assignment as well. At least I have the two people I trust to watch my back and make sure we don't get killed.

"Let the fun begin." Cade's eye twitches with an evil look.

One week later...

We land back at the church exhausted, bruised up, and ready for a shower. Clicking the key fob to unlock the truck, we pile in and slump into the seats. Their trucks were delivered back to their place while we were gone, as the Wolves didn't want attention brought to the church. I'm not sure what makes a difference, with having my truck there versus all three, but who am I to question?

"Let's stop by The Cabin, the restaurant on Parker Street, and get some food. I could also use a nice strong glass of whiskey after this mission," Cade says, swiping a hand down his face.

"I'm down. I also need to meet up with Alex later. She has been a feisty little shit. I need to teach her a lesson about who she's talking to." Cole smirks.

I pulled the truck into the parking lot, putting it into park. We get out of the truck and head toward the front of the restaurant. I look over and see her. I can smell her perfume and hear her sweet laughter. But who the hell is she with?

"What the fuck is Damon doing with Regan? First, he joins the Wolves, and now he goes after your girl. Seems like someone is trying to be you." Cade shakes his head and heads toward the door.

I'm fuming. Who the fuck does he think he is and why is she hanging out with another Wolf? I tell the boys that I'll meet them inside and head back to the truck.

I open the back door and grab my red hoodie and my mask. Tonight, I will claim her. She is mine, and tonight, she'll know. No one else can have her.

I wait in the driver's seat, sending a quick text to the boys that I had to leave, and wait for her to get done. Spotting her exit the restaurant with Damon, I notice she has a smile on her face, leaning into him and giving him a quick hug before departing in the opposite direction. I put the truck in drive with the lights shut off, following her discreetly. As she enters the alley, I follow, trailing her slowly.

Before she turns around, I put the truck in park and jump out. Coming up behind her, she slowly turns. I'm too fast for her, throwing a sack over her head. She thrashes and screams against my hold as I grab her in a tight grip. I slam her against the truck, forcing her hands behind her back, and quickly put a zip tie around her wrist. I pick her up over my shoulder and throw her into the truck.

I pull out of the alley and head toward my penthouse. Luckily, no one was around to spot what I had done. She is screaming and bucking in the backseat.

I pull into the underground parking garage, coming to a stop. She tries to headbutt me as I yank her from the seat.

"Be a good girl and keep quiet, or you will be punished," I growl in her ear.

She goes completely still. Putting her over my shoulder, I enter the elevator and insert my key to take me to the penthouse. As the elevator dings, the doors slide open to my luxurious home.

I enter the foyer and head toward my hidden den. After opening the hidden door, I walk down the hallway to another door. I run my hand up her dress, cupping her sweet pussy in my hand. I push her panties to the side and swipe her sweet cunt with the tips of my fingers. She is already soaking.

She lets out a soft cry, and I smirk with satisfaction. My little spawn is turned on. We haven't even started yet and her body is begging me for more. She has no idea that Satan is playing with her, but she loves it. I set her down on the table, cutting off the zip tie.

Her fist goes flying, looking to connect with my face. I turn her over, slamming her onto the table and smacking her ass. She whimpers. As I maneuver her to her back, I pull her arms over her head, wrapping chains around her wrists. Adding a lock on the end, I click it shut, ensuring she won't escape. I pull the sack from her head, and she takes in her environment, eyes blazing with fury.

"Who the fuck are you? Let me go! This is not funny!" She yanks on the chains above her head. I look down at her, taking in the beauty of her rage. It makes my dick twitch.

"Your wet cunt says otherwise. Basically purring to be touched." I move my hand under her dress, push her panties to the side, and swipe a finger over her pussy, confirming that her juices are flowing, begging to be tasted.

"Let me go. I am not a toy to be played with. I swear to God, I will kill you." Shoving her dress above her waist, I smack her ass and slide her panties off, shoving them into her mouth.

I walk over to my table and grab a mask. Returning to my little spawn, I put it over her eyes. I lean down, flicking my tongue over her wet clit. Jesus, does she fucking taste amazing. I plunge my tongue inside of her, devouring her sweet juices. As I rise from between her legs, she knees me, causing my mask to pierce above my temple.

"I hope you enjoyed that, because that little act earned you a punishment." A growl vibrates from my chest.

I move away from the table, grab my gun, making sure the clip is removed and nothing in the chamber, and shove the barrel into her pussy, pumping it in and out. She cries out in pleasure, taking it so well. She likes this. Oh, my little spawn is going to be my good little slut. As I get her close to her climax, I pull it out of her.

I undo my belt, pushing down my jeans. Sliding out my hard cock, I rub the head along her folds. I pull her to the end of the table, her legs dangling off. I wrap her leg around my hips and slam my cock inside of her tight pussy. Her muffled screams are sweet in my ears as I take her again and again.

Her muscles squeeze against my cock, making me thrust into her harder. I reach up and push the top of her dress down, pinching her nipples and hearing her muffled moans.

She looks so beautiful with her underwear shoved in her mouth, tears running down her face. She enjoys this—the unknown, the domination.

I hit my climax, spilling my seed into her nice and deep. She is mine now, claimed. Her body goes limp and soft snores fill the quiet room. I pull out of her, pulling my jeans back on. Grabbing a washcloth from under the sink, I soak it under warm water, then clean the sweat from her forehead and body. I don't clean my cum, as I want it to leak out of her. I pull her panties back on and unlock the chains.

She is dead weight as I lift her in my arms. I get her back into the truck and take her home. Grabbing her keys out of her purse, we enter through the front door. No one is home, so this will be easy.

I take her into her room, laying her in bed and covering her up. I kiss her on the forehead. Walking over to the window, I open it to make it seem like someone had entered while she was asleep.

"My beautiful spawn, you will be my reckoning," I whisper to her. I shut off the lights, leaving her to rest. She is going to need it for how sore she will be when she wakes up.

Chapter 10

SETH

After leaving Regan's house, I received a call from my father advising me that a meeting has been summoned and I am to attend. I'm assuming it has something to do with new assignments. He didn't say. But he told me to get to the church immediately before disconnecting the line.

Traveling across the gravel, the church comes into view. I find a spot amongst the other vehicles, placing the truck in park. I cut the engine, exiting as the soles to my shoes crunch against the leaves on the ground.

I walk toward the church to catch up to the boys, when I see a shadow charging toward me from the side.

"Who the fuck do you think you are, Seth? Thinking you wouldn't get noticed. I saw you pulling out of the alley where my date entered and suddenly she vanished? Get yourself your own fling and stay away from her." Damon puffs up his chest, acting like I should be scared of him.

Cole and Cade come up by my side, and I throw my head back and laugh. "Oh, Damon. How did you know it was me? Look, you're new here, but Regan has been mine since we were kids. In fact, I had her sweet cunt wrapped around my dick last night, and she enjoyed every moment of it. You are to stay away from her. If I catch you around her again, I will kill you. That's a promise. This is my town. Remember that." I walk past him, shoving his shoulder.

"So, you admit it was you. I know what your truck looks like. We will see about that. She'll forget who you are when I have her cumming for me, screaming my name." I see red. Turning around, I swing, connecting my fist into his jaw. He smiles at me with a bloody mouth and laughs. "Let the best man win."

"Walk away, Seth. We will deal with him. We are 200 feet from the church, with the Elders inside. The last thing you need is for the Elders to see you unhinged over a female." Cade shoves me back toward the church.

I walk into the church, still fuming. Who the fuck does this guy think he is?

As we walk in, the church is packed. This can't be good. I look around, noticing the Elders are gathered on the stage in front of the rows of benches. They settle in their seats along a long table, folding their hands together. As this meeting is not an assignment or a trial, we are not required to wear our masks and hoodies.

We walk up the aisle, sliding into the front row. The crowd becomes silent. My eyes lock with my father's as he nods at me, acknowledging my attendance. Scanning the Elders, I feel the tension oozing from their pores.

"We have a rat in the group. Those who are here are the members we trust with this information. The last thing we need is a riot to start. Someone is going back to the Snakes, giving information about the shipments and hit list. Shipments are going missing, building windows shattered, with Snake graffiti on the walls. They are way too prepared for our arrival. The times, the dates, and the locations of our assignments, in which they escape easily from, and our shipments of weapons are going missing. We need to collect all the information we can get before we turn this into war."

"Kingsley, we need to shut down your club for now. We need to use the chamber for interrogation once we capture those creeping in the shadows. The profits lost during the shutdown will be covered. We have some prospects we suspect, but I want everyone to keep their eyes and ears open. Report anything you find to the Elders."

I nod in agreement. "Just let me know when the club is needed, and it is yours. I would like to attend, considering it is my club. You and I both know I'll be useful getting information."

The Elders glance at each other, nodding in agreement. "We'll send you details when the time comes to shut down."

My mind wanders, thinking who could be stupid enough to cross the Wolves. The only person who comes to mind is Damon.

He is too new to the Empire, along with our town. Popping up out of nowhere, walking in like he owns the place. We don't know who or where he came from. My father looked into him, and all he could find was that he was related to a Wolf, who was an Elder, but had passed away years before the initiation. No one looked deeper into it, but maybe I should. I don't have any proof, but it's a feeling I've had since I first met him.

I glance around the room, noticing he is not in attendance. Why would he come all the way to the church just to size me up, but not actually attend this meeting? He must not have everyone fooled as well as he thinks. I cannot prove his motives for being here, but I will find out. Not only is he trying to stake a claim in my city, but he is also stepping into territory he doesn't belong in.

We continue with the meeting for another hour, discussing business and trades. Once the meeting ends, Cole, Cade, and I get up, heading down the aisle. My father walks over, clapping my shoulder.

"Your mother and I plan on having a dinner party in a couple of weeks. I will send you over details once your mother makes up her mind on a day and time. We would like the three of you to attend, as your parents will be there as well. Bring dates. It is time you boys find your ol' ladies." My dad smirks, walking toward the door.

"Hey, Dad?" I yell after him before he exits. Stopping in his tracks, he turns to face me. "I noticed Damon wasn't in attendance. Was there a reason?"

"We did not see a use for him, therefore he did not get the summons. The three of you attended because you're our children, and we feel that in order to take over our legacy, you need to prove that you can handle bigger matters within the Empire. Don't disappoint me." He turns back around, heading out the door.

If Damon was not part of this meeting, then why did he show up in the parking lot? How did he know I would be here unless he followed me? Knitting my eyebrows together, my train of thought is broken by Cade's whiny voice.

"Great. First, we get this placed on us, then your father had to hit us with the reminder that we need to hurry the fuck up and get ol' ladies," Cade grumbles, shaking his head.

"What's wrong, Cade? Can't keep anyone long enough to put up with your grumpy ass?" Cole laughs, hitting his shoulder.

Shaking my head, I head toward the truck. My mind wanders back to the night I captured Regan—my head between her thighs, the taste of her juices and sounds of her moans. I remember how much she enjoyed it, and her body screaming at me not to stop.At that moment, she was my little slut.

I wanted to stay away from her. I wanted her to stay away from me. This life isn't for her. But after getting a taste of her, I'm addicted. She has me wrapped around her finger, and she doesn't even know it yet.

Chapter 11

Regan

It's early morning as I wake up in my bed. How did I get into my room? I don't remember coming back here. I sit up, my thighs and arms aching. What the fuck did I do? I get out of bed and walk over to the window, looking out and see my truck parked out front. Wait a minute... The window was unlocked and opened. I know for a fact I did not leave this window open.

I walk into my bathroom, and looking into the mirror, I see bruises on my arms. I look down, seeing bruises on my legs. It all comes back to me. The masked Wolf kidnapped me and fucked the shit out of me. In a sick, twisted way, I kind of liked it. It was a huge turn on, but it was familiar. I don't know why, but his hands, his smell, were too familiar.

Maybe that was why I liked it. I wanted to be thrown around like a rag doll. God, I sound like a desperate slut.

The doorbell rings, and I look at the clock. It's eight o'clock in the morning. Who could possibly be here? My parents aren't home, my brother spent the night with his friends, and I know Alex's ass is just waking up like me or not even out of bed yet.

Grabbing my phone, I walk down the stairs and open the door. No one is there. I looked around, not seeing anyone. I swear the doorbell rang. As I go to turn around, I notice a box on the step with my name on it.

I open the box, dropping it instantly. I scream as my whole body starts to tremble. Inside is a dead, bloody crow and a note. Bending over, I pick up the note, unfolding it.

Be a good little whore and stay away from Seth Kingsley.

What the fuck? My phone dings, and I pull it out of my pocket to a text from an unknown number.

Unknown: I hope you loved my gift. This is your first and only warning. Stay away from Seth.

I back away into the house, slamming and locking the door. Turning, I sprint upstairs, locking myself in my room. I run over to the window, shutting it tight and locking it. Entering my closet with the lights off, I slide down to the floor, holding my knees to my chest. Tears rolling down my face, I rock back and forth. My heart is beating a million miles a minute, and I am on the verge of a panic attack. What the fuck is going on? I have only had a short conversation with Seth at the club. Why does this keep happening to me?

After about an hour of being isolated in my closet, without hearing any noises inside the house, I am almost positive no one entered. Getting up, I walk over to my bathroom sink and wash my tear-streaked face. I pull my phone out and send a quick text to Alex that I am coming over.

As I'm driving to Alex's house, my eyes dart to my rearview mirror every few seconds, monitoring to see if I am being followed. I have a tight grip on my steering wheel to stop my trembling hands. Is this how it's going to be from now on? Always looking over my shoulder, wondering when someone is going to come after me and kill me?

I make a left turn, entering the long driveway toward the front of her house. Trees line the drive, with their leaves swaying in the slight breeze. As I come to a stop, a one-story farmhouse comes into my view. Steps lead up to the wrap-around porch with flower boxes lining the rail. The house is painted white with black trim, shutters and a beautiful black door with windows displayed at the top. It has been years since I have been here, but this home projects peace and serenity.

I notice Alex's parents' vehicles are gone, and the only vehicles in the driveway are her silver Mazda and Cole's black truck. Walking up the steps, I open the front door to the smell of eggs and bacon filling the air. As I enter the kitchen, Alex is sitting at the island as Cole is cooking breakfast. She looks over at me and her face drops.

"Regan, you're white as a ghost. Are you okay?" She grabs me, holding me as my body starts shaking. Cole stops what he is doing, looking over at me with a concerned look.

"No, I'm not. I came home to the one safe place I have, just to be threatened. Should have never come home. I should go back to Alabama and never set foot in this fucking town again."

"Okay, stop. You need to tell me what spooked you so badly because this isn't you. Nothing scares you." She looks at Cole as he pulls out three beers, motioning for us to sit. Normally, it would be too early for a beer, but I don't object. I show them the text and a picture of what had been delivered at my door. I take a deep swig of the beer, closing my eyes.

"I barely had a conversation with Seth. What the hell did I do to deserve this?" I sob.

"Just stay with me for a few days. We can have a slumber party like the old days. No one except us will know you're here." Alex grabs my hand and smiles.

"I will look into this, Regan. Whoever this was will pay, and Seth doesn't hate you. He has his reasons for being the way he is. Even so, he'll go to the end of the world to make sure you're safe." He looks deep into my eyes. I can't help but throw my head back and laugh.

"He sure as fuck knows how to show it, huh? The only reason I came back here was because I HAD to. He didn't give a fuck about me then and he doesn't now. He is Satan, and I got caught in the crossfire of Hell for whatever he did for me to be threatened. So, excuse me, but I don't believe a single thing you say." I push past him and Alex, heading out of the room. I need to breathe. I left one hell and came back to another.

What can all of this mean? This can't have anything to do with what I ran from. How would they know who Seth is? Is it possible Seth is in some shit that has me being watched just because I work at his club? No, that can't be it.

Part of my brain is telling me I should just avoid this whole situation and quit the bar. Let my dad win, once again, and go work for him. The other part of my brain doesn't want me to quit. I have had several shifts during the last week. The money is great, and I am actually starting to enjoy myself!

Why me? Karma is laughing in my face right now, and I have no idea why.

I walk out front and sit on the steps, listening to the wind and birds chirping around me. Alex comes out after a few minutes, sitting next to me and wrapping her arms around me as we sit in silence. Why can't we have normal lives with normal families?

"I love you, boo. You are safe." She kisses my head.

Safe. Is that word even real? Is that even a thing in our world?

Chapter 12

UNKNOWN

Pacing back and forth, impatiently waiting for their arrival, my mind goes back to the day she escaped. She thinks she can get away from me, but she'll never truly escape me. My little dove will be back in her cage, and she will never escape again. I will use her, fuck her, and kill her. She thought stabbing me would kill me or keep me away, but her defiance only turned me on, driving me to want her more.

When she escaped, I harbored enough energy to get to my lair. Blood had dripped down my chest, soon spilling onto the floor with every step I took. The pain had only been temporary. My men had quickly grabbed our doctor to assist with my injuries. He pulled the knife out, quickly sewing me up. Within an hour, I had been making calls to my connections in New Orleans, ordering them to keep an eye out for Regan. Several days went by before I received a call from a Wolf. I almost hadn't taken the call from the nasty mutt.

But he informed me he had been initiated, earning his place within their Empire. Little did they know, he would soon be reporting their movements, assignments, and shipments to the Snakes—to me.

I hear footsteps as two shadows appear behind me. I turn around, facing them.

"Updates on Regan?" Pacing along the room, I flip my pocket knife open and shut.

"She is working at a club as a bartender, her father is an Elder of the Wolves, and it looks like she's caught the eye of Seth Kingsley." The man looks over at me like he is bored.

"Who might you be, and what can I do for you?" I look over at the female standing next to the man.

She tilts her head and starts walking toward me, swaying her hips side to side. "I am the one who will be sending your precious little plaything back to you—begging to be by your side," she whispers in my ear.

"What makes you think I need your help?" I smirk at her, stepping away from her nasty breath. But I'd be lying if I said she wasn't attractive.

She throws her head back and laughs. "Because she is protected by the Wolves, and you cannot be seen here or touch her here. But I can. I also want her far away from the one person I long for. So, I can either send her your way, or

I can kill her. That is up to you." Without a second thought, I grab her neck and slam her against the wall.

"You will not kill her. You will get all the information I need. What she is doing, who she is around, and you will track her every move. You do this, you will live and get your prize. If you fail, and she dies before I get my hands on her, you will be on your knees begging me to let you live. Now leave us." I throw her across the room, watching as she gets to her feet and scrambles out the door.

I don't know why I entertained her, especially with her threats of killing my little dove. But she is useful. She can climb into beds, trading for information. It will be less suspicious if a woman is following another than a man following a woman.

I turn to the guy, who is leaning up against the wall. "What do you want?" I eye him; these little rats always want something.

"Revenge. Her little prize is my revenge. I want him dead." He kicks off from the door frame, cracking his knuckles. "She thinks she is going to have him at the end, but that is far from the truth. A kill for a kill, and unfortunately, he'll fall for the Elders' mistake."

"You'll do the same. However, I also want you to keep an eye on the woman you brought with you. Report back to me. When it is the right time, you will bring her to me. I know who you are, who your father is. But you don't seem to remember who I am. But you'll know in due time." I turn from him, pouring a glass of scotch from the small bar in the corner.

He nods, striding out of the room. Run little rats, scurry off to the sewer to do my bidding. Soon, my little dove, you will be back in your pretty cage. I can't wait to hear your screams, like music to my ears. My lips turn up in a grin. There is nowhere you can go, little dove.

Chapter 13

I receive a text in our group chat from Cole, saying he has some important information. I respond, advising the boys to meet at my penthouse. They both have key cards, so they'll come on up once they arrive. It has to be something serious if it needs immediate attention. Maybe it's a lead to figure out who the rat is amongst the Wolves. I pour myself a glass of whiskey as I wait for their arrival, looking out the living room window at the beautiful Louisiana morning sky.

My mind wanders to Regan, to having a taste of her. That was the biggest mistake I've made. Now I crave her, and I've been going insane with need. I swore off anything to do with her years ago, but that little taste has me addicted. I can't help but smirk thinking about when she finds out who was between her legs last night.

The elevator dings, snapping me out of my trance. I get up, turning to meet Cole and Cade as they walk into the foyer, but the look on Cole's face has me stopping dead in my tracks.

"Cole, you look like you are going to be sick. What is going on?" I stare at him, trying to read his face.

"You should sit. It's about Regan—something's happened." My heart starts racing, causing my body to tremble. "She came over to Alex's house looking pretty shaken up. A package was delivered at her door with a bloody dead crow and a note in it. A threatening text was sent to her from an unknown number, telling her to stay away from you." He shakes his head, sitting on the bar stool.

"The girl is spooked. She is staying at Alex's house right now, but I don't think it is a good idea for her to go home, considering it was delivered there. I don't know who would have the balls to deliver this message, especially with who her dad is. Someone must be watching her. I can't think of anyone you pissed off who would send her the threat. You've barely said a few words to each other since she's been back."

Throwing my whiskey glass at the wall, glass shatters to the floor. I am seething. No one messes with me. How could she get caught in any crossfire? I'm seeing red. This fucker is a dead man walking. Pacing around the room, I try to collect my thoughts, but it isn't working. It's pissing me off even more. Then an idea comes to mind; the only thing I can do that will ensure her safety.

"We will be moving her here, where I can watch her every move. And if I am not here, she will have guards with her at all times. With me, she'll be protected. All these years, I thought I could keep her away from this shit, but I was wrong." I stop pacing, turning to Cole.

"And how are you going to do that, Seth? The girl thinks you hate her, and I'm pretty sure she hates your guts. What, you think she is going to be ecstatic about being forced to live here? Good luck with that." He has a mischievous grin on his face that I want to knock off of his face.

"That is exactly what I am going to do. My little spawn has no choice in this matter. Let's go get her. This needs to be done now before anything else happens." Walking out of the foyer, we take the elevator down to the garage. She isn't going to agree, but she doesn't get a say. She can fight me all she wants, but little does she know, I like when she's feisty. My cock twitches at the thought of her putting up a fight. Maybe now that she'll be living with me, I can finally have another taste of her. This is not the time to get a hard on, and I have to remember I'm doing this for her safety. Taking a deep breath, I crack my neck to the side, trying to release the tension.

I send a quick text to my housekeeper to get the guest room set up and bathroom essentials needed for the night. The boys and I will gather her things tomorrow. I also ask her to clean up the glass so Regan doesn't see me as the same kind of monster that is threatening her.

Making a quick call to her father, I advise him of the threat and tell him I will be taking her to my house. They need to figure out security and who could have dropped the package off without being seen. He agreed, of course—not like he had a damn choice. Elder or not, it's been proven she is not safe there as of now. He seems to think the box has something to do with the rat.

The boys are going through Regan's security footage from this morning on their phones as we head over to Alex's house. They can't seem to find the clip where the package was dropped off. There is a clip of me leaving her house, and then it skips to her discovering the item. Looking at the timestamps, they notice a section of ten hours has been wiped.

Huffing in frustration, I take a breath and keep my eyes on the road, trying to keep my rage in check. The last thing I want is for her to fear me as soon as I walk through the door.

We take a quick detour, heading to the club to drop off Cade. I need someone there, making sure the club is running smoothly, as I deal with this situation. The last thing I need is for issues to occur while I'm out.

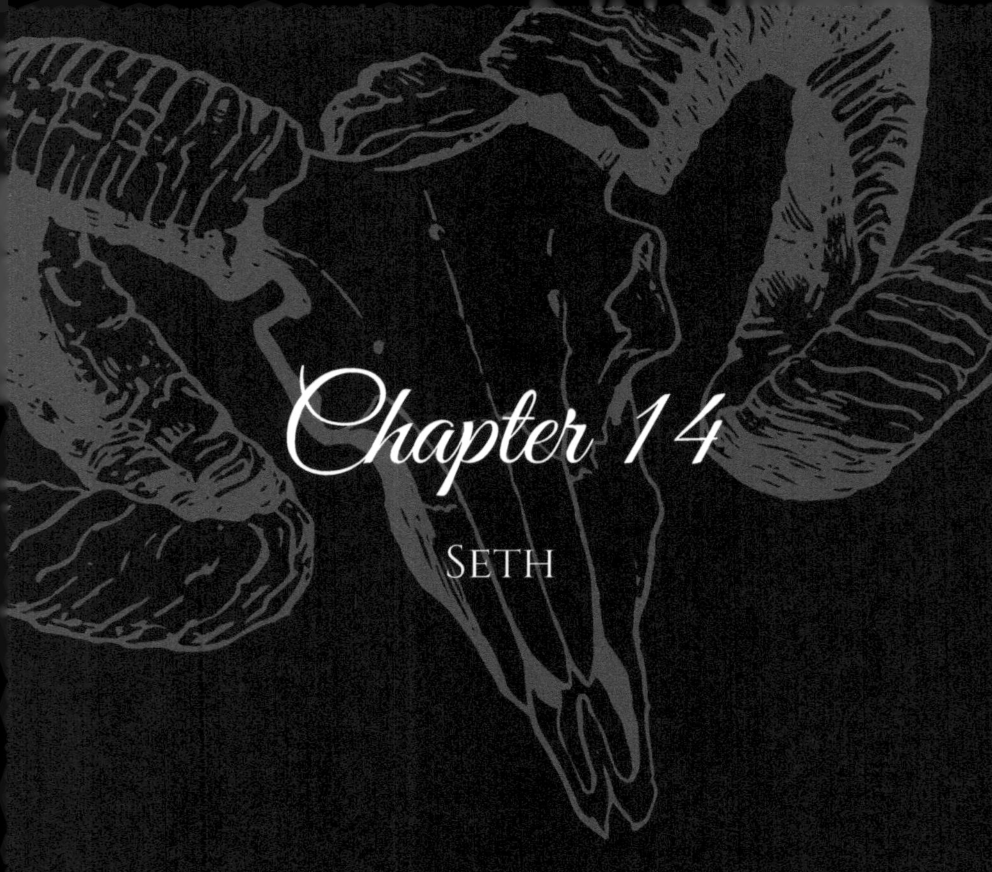

Chapter 14

Seth

It's one in the afternoon when I pull the truck up to Alex's. I get out of the truck and quickly head toward the house. We walk in and find Regan and Alex on the couch watching a movie. I lean up against the wall with arms across my chest, watching them from behind. Cole shuts the door, and the girls jump up from the couch and spin around. Regan screams at the sight of me.

"What is he doing here? You didn't tell him, did you?" She's throwing daggers at Cole.

"Hello to you, too, my little spawn. You aren't happy to see me?" I smirk at her, looking her up and down. She's wearing booty shorts and an oversized tee, which I can see her nipples through. My cock twitches again.

"First of all, I am not your spawn. Second off, you can keep your eyes to yourself. Third of all, I'm out. I am not going to be in the same room as you. You have caused enough problems for me." She slips on her Vans and grabs her purse, pushing past me.

I grab her by the wrist and yank her back. I press my lips against her ear. "That is where you are wrong, my little spawn. You are mine. This is my business, considering it involves me." I lick the side of her face and watch her eyes go big.

"Let me the fuck go, Seth. I know you like to play games, but this isn't a game, and I want no part of it. So, you can kindly fuck off." She tries to yank her wrist free, but I hold on tight. I grab her by the waist and throw her over my shoulder.

I start to walk toward the door with her kicking, thrashing, and screaming. I smack her sweet ass and smirk over at Cole.

"See, I love playing games, sweetheart, and the game we are about to play is going to be fun. Considering you are being threatened at your own home and most likely being watched, you will be going home with me, so I can keep an eye on you. I will send Cole and Cade to get your things."

"Seth, put me down now. I am not going home with you. You are out of your fucking mind!" she screams and hits me right in the throat.

I put her down, and she tries to make a run for it, but I grab her and slam her against the wall. I have my hand wrapped around her throat, leaning into her and taking her scent in.

"How about you be a good girl and do as you are told or I am going to fuck the disobedience out of you right here until you beg me to stop?" I watch her eyes widen; tears roll down her face as I squeeze her neck. She nods in agreement, and I let go of her. Grabbing her hand, I guide her out the door and walk over to my truck.

"Cole will follow us with your truck, and you will ride with me, little spawn." I smirk at her as she stomps over to the truck, getting into the passenger side and slamming the door.

"Well, that went smoothly. Maybe she will set your house on fire next with the way she is throwing daggers your way." Cole kisses Alex and heads toward Regan's truck as I toss the keys at him.

Sliding into the truck, I start it up. In my peripheral vision, I see her curled up in the passenger's seat, pressed against the door. She is furious, but soon she'll understand this is to protect her from whoever is threatening her because of me. I will find out who is doing this, and they will burn.

"So, what happens now? Am I supposed to live locked up with you like a good little girl? What about my family? They will know I am not living at the house." She glares at me, cracking her knuckles.

"It will be handled. You will continue working at the bar and ride with me there every day. You will come back to the penthouse, and that is where you will stay until I figure out who sent you the threat."

"Why do you care? You made it very clear years ago that I wasn't shit to you." She rolls her eyes and huffs.

"Can't you just say thank you?" Staring ahead, I click the volume tab on my steering wheel, indicating that I am done with this conversation.

We remain silent on the way home. Thank God for the music playing to drown out the tension.

Traveling down the busy street, tourists fill the sidewalk, going in and out of the different shops. We make a right onto Parker Street and my building comes into view. The building's exterior is black, with windows lining the structure for each apartment. The building is eight stories high, providing an amazing view of the city. There is a valet who waits at the front to take the residents' vehicles. I don't ever utilize him, as I need to know exactly where my vehicle is parked at all times. Making another right further down the street, I drive down into the underground parking.

We pull into my spot, and I get out, shutting the door. I walk around to the passenger side to get her and we walk to the elevator together. I pull out my card, swiping it on the scanner to gain access. The elevator opens and we step in. After pressing the penthouse button, we wait in silence as I look down at my phone, texting Cade to see how the club is doing. She's quiet. She is never this quiet, and I want to know what she is thinking. The elevator comes to a stop and dings, indicating that we've reached the top. The doors open, and I motion her forward, following behind.

I set her purse on the counter and walk over to the fridge. I pull out two waters and toss her one. She catches it, but doesn't look at me.

"Marie will be here in the morning. She takes care of the space and will have breakfast ready for you in the morning. If you need anything washed, just put it in the hamper in the bathroom and it will be done. You have your own bathroom in the guest bedroom, and it is always stocked with toiletries. Your new work uniform will be here in the morning, and your things will be here when you get off work." I walk toward her bedroom, and she follows. I open the door and show her in. She hesitates at first but walks in, looking around.

"I can take care of myself. I don't need you to hire someone," she scolds as she looks around the room.

"I didn't hire her just for you, princess. She has been with me for years. When she is here, I suggest you let her proceed with her business. She doesn't take kindly to being told no. She is a nice lady, so be nice." Then I brush past her to the door.

"I am nice. I just don't like you," I hear her huff with annoyance.

"If you need anything, I'm across the penthouse." I shut the door, letting her have her space. We will see how long it takes before she tries to make a run for it. I'll give it an hour.

I walk into my room, take off my suit jacket, and toss it on the chair that sits in the corner. Striding across the room and into the bathroom, I turn the shower to hot and peel off my clothes. Today has been a long fucking day. Stepping under the spray, bowing my head forward, I let the steaming water pour down my body. The scorching water relaxes my muscles, as my mind goes a hundred miles an hour.

Regan

Walking into the penthouse, I notice that the floor plan is open. To the right is a sizable open kitchen with an island in the middle, a double-door fridge, and stainless steel appliances. There is a door off to the side that might be a pantry. Across from the kitchen is a dark gray sectional that looks way too comfy. In front of the couch is a TV that I swear takes up half of the wall. On either side of the TV, there are leather lounge chairs, and the walls have art portraits that are black and white. One of them looks like it is in a forest with some sort of cabin. The floors are hardwood with a deep rustic finish.

I follow Seth into the guest bedroom, and I'm shocked at its massive and luxurious size to be in a penthouse. There is a king-sized bed with a comforter that looks like a cloud, as though I could sink into it and let it swallow me into nothingness. The room light is dimmed but looks like it is controlled by a remote on the wall next to the enormous TV on the wall. There are two doors; one is opened, in which I can see is the bathroom, and another that I assume is a closet. If this is the guest bedroom, I wonder what the master bedroom looks like. My mind wanders to if I might ever be invited into that room as I embrace his scent lingering in the air. What the fuck, Regan? I shake my head. Why am I thinking that way? I must be going crazy with everything that has gone on today. He gives me the rundown and walks out, closing the door.

I take a deep breath. I need to get out of here and get home. He can't keep me here, and he sure as hell doesn't own me. I'll wait until he goes to bed and then make my escape. Can't help but wonder how worried my parents are. I heard my father talking to someone in his office about a Snake just the other day. He probably thinks the Snakes kidnapped me and it's only a matter of time before he assigns all available Wolves to retrieve me. What will he do to Seth when he finds out he's the one who took me?

I spend the next ten minutes looking around. The closet is a walk-in that would hold all my clothes times two, but currently sits empty. The bathroom has an oversized garden tub that could fit at least three people and a walk-in shower off to the side that has a waterfall shower head hanging from the ceiling. There is a vanity area with a mirror and lights, along with a long counter and a sink with a bronze faucet. I wander out of the bathroom, finding myself standing at the floor to ceiling windows, looking over the town, when my stomach growls.

It's now that I remember that I haven't eaten anything besides the popcorn while Alex and I were watching X-Men.

I quietly open the door and tiptoe my way to the kitchen. As I round the corner, I freeze when I see Seth closing the fridge. He's wearing nothing but gray sweats, which allows me a better look at the tattoos that cover his entire top half. This is the first time I notice just how fit and toned he actually is, his solid six pack on full display. The image of him has my body tingling, and I know my panties are soaked.

My eyes trail back up his body, and a small gasp escapes my throat when our eyes lock. His hand brushes through his wet hair and a grin slowly creeps up his cheeks. Fuck, he totally caught me checking him out.

"Like what you see, little spawn?" He looks me up and down, clicking his tongue.

"Whatever helps you sleep at night." I change the subject as I walk to the door that I believe is the pantry. "I was just coming to find a snack, or is that not allowed?"

I reach for the handle with my brain shouting, "Please be a pantry; please be a pantry." The last thing I need is to further embarrass myself. Thankfully, when I open the door, I find not only a pantry, but one that is fully stocked with... wait, are those my favorite childhood snacks? I grab a bag of Hot Cheetos and confirm my previous thought.

He's suddenly at my back, and I feel his breath on my ear. "I am not going to starve you, but I can give you some fuel if that is what you are wanting."

I push past him, because if I don't, I will give in and let that sexy man fuel me all night long. But I can't. I hate him, and he hates me, and I am not looking to get into something toxic again. Hell, it's already toxic because he is holding me against my damn will.

"Goodnight." I walk into my room and close the door.

It is about 12 a.m. and the house is quiet. He has to be asleep by now. I climb out of bed, slipping on my shoes quietly. Fuck, my truck keys and purse are on the counter. I have my light off so that no light seeps into the house. Slowly, I open my door and tiptoe out of my room. I look across and his door is shut, the lights to the kitchen are off, and it is dead quiet. Perfect, now is my chance. I spot my purse and truck keys. Slowly and quietly, I grab them, heading toward the elevator. I hear a click and then he clears his throat.

"Going somewhere, my little spawn? I am a little disappointed; you took longer than I thought." His deep voice booms in the quiet room. My heart drops. Son of a bitch.

Chapter 15

Regan

I turn around as the lights click on and see him sitting in one of the leather lounge chairs in the living room. He's sitting there, yet again shirtless, with a glass in his hand. I have to get out of here. I am closer to the elevator than he is to me. If I don't leave soon, he'll tear me apart. I spin around and book it to the elevator. I don't even hear him get up before I feel his hand in my hair, yanking me back. He throws me up against the wall, hand still in my hair. He yanks my head back, my scalp burning with the hold he has on it.

"So, you thought I was stupid enough to think you wouldn't try to leave? Tell me, Regan, have you ever danced with the Devil?" He licks the side of my face. My legs instantly clench together. I can feel myself getting wet. I try to get out of his hold by kicking out, but his grip goes tighter around me.

"Seth, you cannot hold me captive. You are no better than the one sending me threats." I spit on him, shooting daggers like they are going to save me from this beast.

He wipes my spit with a single finger and then sticks his fingers in his mouth, sucking my spit onto his tongue. My body is trembling. I know my underwear is soaked. Oh fuck, I am fucked with the look he has in his eyes. I am pinned against the wall, one of his hands keeping me in place by my wrists above my head, while the other trails down my side. He slides his hand into my shorts and cups my pussy. I thrash, trying to escape his grip.

"Mmmm, so wet for me," he breathes into my ear. He rubs my folds with his thumb. A moan slips through my lips. I continue to try to get out of his grasp, but he pins me tighter. He plunges his thick fingers inside of me, pumping in and out. I can feel myself becoming hotter and hotter as he pumps inside of me faster. "Cum for me, my little spawn," he growls.

And that's all it takes to make me go over the edge. I sag in his hands, and he pulls his fingers out of my shorts, bringing them to his lips. He sucks my cum, every last drop, and pulls his fingers out of his mouth with a pop.

"You fix that fucking attitude. Don't make me correct you again." His searing breath vibrates against my ear, causing me to shiver. Letting me go, he picks me up, taking me to my bedroom. He sets me on my bed and leaves the room.

That's it? He's just going to walk out after what he just did? After he took advantage of me? I lie there, taking deep breaths. The Devil has made his point. He is always one step ahead, holding all the control. He is not going to let me out of his reach.

I wake up in a panic as a cloth bag goes over my head. Screaming, kicking and trying to get away, but I feel strong hands on me. I'm flipped onto my stomach, my hands yanked behind me and shoved to my back. I hear a zip, plastic piercing my skin. My hands are bound tight. No. No, this cannot be happening. Did he find me? I'm picked up and thrown over a shoulder. Panicking, my body starts to shake as a scream creeps out of my mouth. I think I'm going to pass out.

A creek sound fills the silent room as a door opens, then shuts, and I am thrown onto a metal-like table, or at least that's what it feels like when I hit my fucking head. The cloth is pulled from my head, and I blink, trying to take in the room. It's dark, with red lights going up the walls. I see a figure in the corner wearing a red hoodie, hiding their head, and when he turns around, there is that wolf mask. Oh, fuck, he is back. The one who took me a couple days ago from the alley.

"Please, don't do this. Let me go." Tears go down my face. I am shaking. Is he going to kill me?

A deep voice rings through the room. "Be a good girl and open your mouth." He is now in front of me with something in his hands. I do as he says, because what other option do I have? He places a ball in my mouth and secures a strap around my head. Oh, fuck, is this a ball gag?

He pulls a knife from his back pocket, and a muffled scream escapes me as I'm kicking out, thrusting my body to get off the table. He grabs my hands and cuts the zip tie. As soon as I get my hands free, I slap him. A growl like laughter comes from his lips. He grabs my arms and puts them over my head, slamming my back on the table. He chains my hands and moves down to my legs to tie them wide the fuck open with leather straps. God, I'm soaking wet. I shouldn't be, and maybe that makes me sick.

He leans over and cuts my shirt open, running the tip of the blade down my chest, barely touching. A shiver courses down my body. He hooks the front of my bra with the knife, and it falls to each side in half. Cupping my breast in his hand and leaning down, sucking gently at first, but then in a deep suck, he licks around the nipple and bites hard. A cry comes out of my mouth, tears rolling down my face. He moves down to my shorts and rips them off.

"Look at you, dripping wet for me already. You like being a little slut for me." He leans over, licking my folds slowly, and then plunges his tongue inside me. A moan creeps out and my body starts to heat. He eats me out so roughly, but it's so good. He stops, and I try to beg him not to, but I'm muffled by the gag. Drool is running down my face at this point with the ball in my mouth.

He grabs the knife again, and instantly I'm screaming in terror. I'm going to be cut open. This is how I go. Tied up, with a ball gag in my mouth. At least I got some pleasure out of it. He flips the knife over so the blade is facing him and the thick handle is facing my way. He plunges the handle inside my cunt, thrusting in and out.

"You will take this like the good little slut you are. Look at you drip all over the handle." He's pumping in and out of me fast and hard. I'm shaking, and I know I'm about to climax. He pulls the knife out and slaps my throbbing pussy. He shoves his fingers back inside, finishing me off. I cum all over his fingers. He looks up, his mask hiding the majority of his face, and he has a grin spread across his face. He sticks his fingers in his mouth, taking every last drop. A moan escapes him. "You taste like I am going to Hell and sweetness." My eyes become heavy. After the series of events today, this has really driven me to exhaustion. My eyes shut and I slip into oblivion.

I wake up dizzy, my eyes blurry, and I have no idea where I am. Blinking a couple of times to clear my vision, I realize that I'm back in my room under the covers, wearing a T-shirt and pajama shorts. I'm confused. This wasn't what I was wearing when I went to bed.

My body hurts like I was hit by a train. I look down at my arms, and there are bruises around my wrist. Pushing the covers off, looking down at my legs, I see handprint marks on my thighs and dark circles around my ankles. I think back and wonder. Did last night really happen? Who was that and how did they get into Seth's penthouse?

I push off the bed and head into the bathroom. Switching on the light, I find a box with my bathroom stuff on the floor. I step back out of the bathroom and notice boxes with my things around the room. How hard did I sleep? I didn't hear one sound. Walking back into the bathroom, I turn on the shower and get undressed as I wait for the water to heat up.

I step under the showerhead and stand there as water sprays down on me, not moving. The hot water feels amazing around my tight muscles, causing them to relax. I try to remember everything that happened last night, but it is just a blur. The only evidence of anything happening is these marks. I must be going absolutely insane.

I was shoved down a rabbit hole and don't know if I will survive. That's the sick thrill, right? Enjoy the dive because I have a feeling there is more that I can't remember, but some things I will never forget.

Chapter 16

Regan

Emerging from my bedroom freshly showered and dressed, ready to give Seth a piece of my mind, but it is so quiet that you could hear a pin drop. I walk over to the kitchen, looking in the fridge, and grab a Dr. Pepper. Cracking it open, I take a deep swig, letting the bubbles burn down my throat. Walking over to the pantry, I swing it open to see if I can find something to eat, as my stomach is screaming at me. I pick my poison and sit down at the island. It's 11 a.m., and I have never slept in like this. I close my eyes and take a deep breath. It's okay, Regan, everything will work out, I keep telling myself. Opening my eyes, I see a note on the table.

> *Headed to the office. Cade will be here to*
> *pick you up at 4 for your shift. Be ready.*
> *P.S. Don't try to run. I have guards waiting*
> *downstairs, my little spawn.*

Great, an escort and bodyguards. I finish what I am eating and head back into my room. I guess I better unpack, since there is no use trying to escape, as he seems to be one step ahead of me. There is no use in fighting him on this matter, but that doesn't mean I am going to bow down to everything. Sighing, I start unpacking my clothes, putting some into the dresser, and walk over to the closet. I find a stereo and crank up the music, blasting Bad Omens' new album.

After a couple of hours of getting unpacked, I hear my phone ding. Well, I guess he didn't take that away from me. I go into my purse and see that Alex texted me.

Alex: I hope you know this was not my idea,
and I had nothing to do with it.

Me: I know, it's fine. At least I
won't die here... Maybe

Alex: Maybe he will let you have a girls' night,
and we can have a sleepover and
eat a bunch of junk food.

Me: He has no say. Do you work tonight at the club?

Alex: Yes, see you at 4. xoxo

I throw my phone back into my purse and go over to the closet, grabbing an outfit for tonight. I get dressed and head into the bathroom to do my hair and makeup. After about thirty minutes, I walk out and put on my checkered Vans. I hear a ding from the elevator, alerting me that someone is here. Glancing at the clock, it is already 3:15. Walking out of my room and closing the door, I look up to see a tall, muscular, tattooed male with a short, thick beard. Damn, if all his little pets look like that, I could get used to being escorted.

"Good to see you again, Regan. We have to get going, so I would hurry your ass up." He turns around, heading back to the elevator.

"First, I have never seen you before. And second, you can learn to be nice instead of being one of his minions and acting like you're tough shit." I walk past him, hitting his shoulder.

"You are a feisty little thing, aren't you? Seth sure as shit has his hands full with you. We've met before; we went to school together." I roll my eyes, not remembering this guy at all. He stands there in the foyer, scanning the premises.

"Now, who is the slow ass? Will you hurry up? I'm going to be late for my shift, and then YOU will have to deal with Satan himself." He shakes his head, walking into the elevator. Once we get to the bottom, sure as shit, there they are. Tall, sexy, tattooed gods who are there to keep me hostage. We walk out of the complex, and I notice that Cade has a Ford Power Stroke in a burgundy color, with a four-inch lift. I have to pull myself up with the oh shit bar since I'm so short. On the way to the club, it is a quiet twenty-minute ride. Good.

The club doesn't open for another hour, but we get there early to help set up and make sure the barbacks get everything we need. The lights are on, and it's quiet other than the noise of glasses clinking. I walk up the bar, about to pull the island door up to enter, but pause. "Seth wants to see you in his office before you start," Chris says, without looking up at me. Of course he does.

I walk over to the elevator and click the button to his office. The elevator leads up, and the door opens to a hallway. Stepping out, I look around the hallway walls, lined with black and white photos of wolves and the forest, but what causes me to pause is the demon nun. That's not creepy. I walk up to the door and knock. I hear his movements and the door swings open. Standing in front of me is Seth, wearing a black button-down shirt tucked into his black dress pants, with a black belt that almost blends in. His sleeves are rolled neatly, exposing his hand and arm tattoos, with bulky rings on his fingers. He is wearing dress shoes, and his hair is slicked back. Jesus, he is fucking gorgeous.

He clears his throat. "Like what you see, little spawn? Come in. Your new uniform is folded on the couch." He turns and walks back to his desk. He sits down so gracefully it reminds me of the slow motion clips of Baywatch girls running on the beach.

"Chris didn't tell me there was a dress code, and I didn't have one before." Looking at the pile, I pick it up, noticing that my new 'uniform' is black booty shorts, wide cross fishnet stockings, and a V-cut tank top.

"Last time I checked, Chris isn't the owner of this club. Put it on." He eyes me with intensity.

"Do you have a bathroom I can change in, then?" I pick up the scraps of clothing.

"Get dressed right there. No one can see you through the window." He looks me up and down as if he can see right through my clothes.

"And I asked if you had a bathroom, in case you are hard of hearing." I fold my arms over my chest, tapping my foot, waiting for him to point me in the direction.

"Regan, if you don't get dressed right here right now, I will rip your damn clothes off and dress you myself." He's challenging me, and my gut is telling me he would do exactly that. I huff and take off my shoes and pull down my shorts, slowly exposing my ass. I can still feel him watching me, but I try to ignore it and play a little cocky.

I slowly pull the fishnets over my legs, propping my foot on the coffee table. Once they are on, I slide the booty shorts over my ass and bend down, ass toward him, putting my shoes on. This is a little payback for the shit he pulled, leaving me needy. God, why am I like this, and what is my problem? I hate him, but I feel the need to tease him. I take my shirt off, exposing my boobs that are nearly spilling out of my bra, and slide the tank top over my head.

I turn around and nearly run into his chest and screech. How the fuck did he move? I didn't even hear him. He grabs me, pulling me close to him.

"That was very naughty of you, my little spawn. Seems like you want to be punished again," he growls into my ear.

Shit, I'm fucked. I played this game knowing that I wouldn't win.

Chapter 17

SETH

My little spawn wants to play games now. She can have her moment, but Satan is here, and he wants to play.

Pulling her into my chest, I spin her around and pin her back to me, my left arm across her chest as my right hand slides down the front inside of her pants. I can feel her shaking, but her hands instantly come up to my arm across her chest. Rubbing her folds in a circle, I can feel that she is already wet for me. I plunge two fingers inside of her and pump them in and out. She starts breathing heavily.

"You like this? You like me inside of you?" I whisper in her ear. She nods her head, and I thrust my fingers harder into her. She's close to her climax, but I will not let her finish—not now. I pull out my fingers and let go of her chest.

She spins around, looking at me with fire in her eyes. "What the fuck, Seth? Is this a game to you? Is that all I am to you, just like the old days?"

I stick my fingers in my mouth, staring into her eyes, and suck every last drop of her juices. Walking over to my desk and opening a drawer, I pull out Ben Wa Balls.

"Oh baby girl, this isn't over. Come here and bend over my desk." She walks over to me, eyeing what I hold in my hands. She bends over and I pull her shorts and fishnets down. I smack her nice, juicy ass and she yelps. "Spread your legs and be still." She does as she is told, like the good little slut she is. I rub her folds again, sticking my finger back in for a couple more thrusts before pulling back out. I suck on the balls, covering them with my saliva and shovel them into her pussy.

"What the fuck did you just put inside of me? Take it the fuck out." She whips around, trying to stick her hand to her pussy to pull it out.

I yank her hand, shoving her back onto my desk. She stares up at me with fear in her eyes. "You will keep those in until I tell you. You are to clench your pussy all night, making sure they don't fall out. You will then come back to my office after your shift is over. Do you understand me?" She nods her head, bending down to pull her fishnets and shorts back up her legs. She exits my office, closing the door behind her.

I sit back at my desk, leaning back in my chair and thinking about all the ways I will have her. I undo my belt, unzipping my pants, pulling out my hard cock. Desperate for a release, but I won't have anyone but her. Stroking my cock, slowly at first, and then picking up the speed, pumping up and down my shaft, picturing her bent over my desk as I pound into her tight pussy. After several minutes, I find my release. Getting up, I go into the bathroom in my office and clean up. I walk out, fastening my belt, and sit in my chair. I turn on the TV on my office wall, monitoring the cameras so I can keep an eye on her. I want to see if she will be a good girl and do as she is told.

This girl is going to be my downfall, but I am willing to fall to my knees if that means she is mine and only mine.

Regan

I walk into the elevator, still in a daze with what just happened. How could I let that happen with the person I despise the most? Again, at that. I curse at my body for liking it. For wanting more and for him to finish me off. My panties are soaked in my juices, and these balls inside of me don't make it any better. How am I going to keep these things in and be able to stand this need to get off that is coursing through my body?

The elevator dings, announcing that I am back on the main floor, which brings me out of my daze. I head into the bathroom to make sure my hair and makeup are presentable. Observing myself in the mirror, inspecting, but finding that everything is still in place. As I turn on the faucet and start washing my hands, I hear a toilet flush. I mind my own business and grab a paper towel to dry my hands.

I turn around and see a woman standing there with a smirk on her face. "Welcome back, Regan. Seems like daddy didn't want you to work for them after all, so you had to turn into a bar slut. What, did daddy cut your allowance off?" She walks over to the sink and washes her hands.

"Morgan. Nice to see your attitude never changes. What I do and where I work is none of your business. And my daddy doesn't want me working here. He has an open position for me, but I chose to do something I like. I hope you have the day you deserve." I turn to walk out of the bathroom to head to the bar.

"You know, while you've been gone, Seth moved on. He's been fucking me every day since you left. I give him what he needs—too bad you couldn't do that when you had the chance. In fact, I am heading up to his office now."

She smirks at me, bumping into my shoulder before leaving out the door.

Desperate slut. Why would I give a fuck what Seth did while I was gone? We weren't together, and he made it very clear he gave no fucks about me. But a thought goes through my head. Why the fuck would he finger fuck me and stick this shit inside of me when he has her coming to his office right after? My anxiety kicks in. Maybe I really am nothing to him but a play toy he enjoys torturing. Why is my heart wanting more of him? Why are feelings creeping back when I want them to be dissolved completely? Yeah, no. Fuck that. I walk out of the bathroom with my head held high, pushing out with confidence. This will not weaken me; I will not kneel for anyone or be anyone's play toy.

As I head out toward my station, Alex comes up to me, giving me a quick hug as she balances a tray of shots. Looks like she is the shot girl tonight. As she turns, I give her a playful smack as she prances off to sell shots to the group of guys.

It's been three hours since I started my shift, and the club is busy. Chris and I split the bar into two sections for each of us to work. I pour shots of gummy bear for the girls who are being flirtatious with the guys next to them and tequila shots for the guys who are making the girls chase them in circles. They are totally going home together tonight.

I wipe down the bar, cleaning up the spilled drinks and stacking up clean cups the barbacks brought to us.

I can feel a looming presence standing in front of me. I am about to look up and ask what I can get them when I see a tall, muscular man smiling down at me. "Hey, beautiful. I haven't heard from you since our dinner. I was beginning to think you were avoiding me."

"Hey, Damon. I'm sorry I haven't reached out in a couple of days. I've been busy, not avoiding you, I promise." I smile at him. "What can I get ya?"

"A second date would be good and a Coors." He leans over the bar toward me, making me freeze for no reason at all. This guy is so damn nice, and I really had a good time with him, so why am I hesitating to say yes right away? Handing him his beer, I say, "I had a really good time with you. I'm a little busy, but I will see when my schedule comes out and let you know." I smile sweetly at him.

"Sounds good. Maybe we can get out of this town, since there is not much here. There is a carnival coming up a town over." Picking up his beer and taking a deep swig, I eye him. Yeah, I don't know if I can just go to another town with Seth breathing down my neck, and I also don't feel comfortable leaving the protection of the Wolves.

I nod my head in acknowledgement and head over to the new customers that just approached. I can feel him staring at me. Honestly, I am a little freaked out. I shake it off and step farther down the bar to avoid another conversation.

HE has ruined me for any chance of thinking a man can be good to me. HE is the reason I am back in this town trying to lie low.

It's finally closing time for the club, and my feet are killing me. We close out all the tabs, count our money, and turn everything in. The tips were flowing tonight. I was so busy I forgot about the balls and that I had to go up to Seth's office after my shift. Dread fills me at the thought of returning, but I really need to get this over with because I'm done after this. I have other things to worry about than being his plaything, and he's apparently with Morgan. That's a big hell no for me. I will not be his sidepiece.

Chapter 18

SETH

I am nose deep into paperwork, and I've completely lost track of time, between getting texts from the Elders, doing some scans of the town for suspicious activity, and finally getting some club business done. I hear a knock at the office door, and I look up at the clock. The club is closed; it has to be Regan.

The door opens and Regan walks in looking exhausted, but I also see a hint of irritation on her face. She strolls in, closing the door, turning back around to shoot daggers at me. I don't know what crawled up her sweet ass, but I want a piece of it.

"I'm done with my shift; I kept these things in all night. Can I take them out now so we can go back to the penthouse?" she huffs, standing there with her arms across her chest.

I get up and walk over to her, running my hand down her face. She flinches. What the fuck is that about? "Place your hands against the wall and bend over."

"I can do it myself, Seth. I will just use your bathroom." She starts to walk past me when I stop her, grabbing her arm.

"I didn't ask, my little spawn. Now bend over and put your hands against the wall, or I'll force you to." Her eyes go big and she mutters under her breath, bending over and doing exactly as I say. I pull down her shorts and fishnets, pushing her legs wider. I rub my thumb across her folds, causing her to shutter, then slide my finger in, removing the balls. They fall to the floor with a small thud. What a good girl. She kept them in, exactly as I told her to.

She starts to push off the wall to rise, but I quickly push her back to the wall. I can't control myself any longer. I need her. I need to bury myself deep inside of her.

"*Seth,*" she whimpers as I slide my fingers in and out of her. With my other hand, I undo my belt and unzip my pants. I pull my hard cock out, stepping up against her. I rub my head along her wet folds, soaking me with her juices. Slowly pushing into her, she starts to squirm and pushes herself against me. I wrap her hair around my hand and pull her head back. I slam into her, thrusting hard and fast.

A moan creeps from her mouth and her breathing picks up.

"Seth, don't stop. Harder. I need you," she begs. I thrust in her deeper and faster as she screams my name. Her muscles tighten around me as she cums all over my cock. I pump a few more times before I find my release. As I pull out, she slumps against the wall.

"Clean it up, little spawn." She starts to go to the bathroom, but I stop her. "Get on your knees and lick every drop. I want you to taste how good we are." She hesitates, but she gets on her knees, grabbing my shaft. She looks up at me, staring into my eyes, and licks every drop of our release.

Fuck, that's hot. I didn't think she would listen. Once she's done, I pick her up and move her to the couch. I spread her legs wide for me and get on my knees, and I flip my tongue up her sweet folds. She tastes amazing, and I don't waste one drop.

I stand up, buckling my belt as she pulls up her fishnets and shorts. She looks away toward the wall, holding her arms. I want to be in her head. I want to know what she is thinking. Does she feel the pull to me as I do her? My phone rings and I look down, seeing it's my father, and answer.

"Seth, the Elders need you at the church. We have business to discuss. Bring the boys."

"Give me thirty minutes and I'll be there." Hanging up the phone, I send the boys a quick text to meet in my parking garage and shove it into my pocket.

"I'll take you home, then I have some business to take care of." I walk past her with an indifferent face, not wanting her to see that I had any satisfaction from what we did—not yet. I want her to beg for me.

We get to the penthouse, and she gets out of the car. I see one of my guards walking up and I nod. They step into the elevator, and I can see the glare she gives the guard as the door shuts. I wait and watch the elevator until it hits the penthouse.

Cade and Cole appear at the truck, Cole jumping in the front seat and Cade in the back.

"Have any idea what this is about? They have any intel about the Snakes?" Cade asks from the back with his arms spread wide against the back of the seat.

"No idea, but we're about to find out." I put the car in drive and screech out of the parking garage.

As we arrive at the church, I see my father's vehicle at the front. We park and get out of the truck, walking toward the doors. As I approach the doors, I see my father.

"Masks on, hoods up, boys. We have two men chained up in the basement. We need them moved and brought back to the club." We do as we are told; I make sure my pistol is tucked at my back waistband before walking inside to the stairs.

We climb down the stairs into the dark room with dimmed lights. We see two men chained up and bloodied against the wall.

"Wolves, you sons of bitches," the one on the left screams. I pull out my pistol and slam the hilt of it against his head and he slouches. The other one starts thrashing, and I do the same to him. Cade walks over to the left and unclips the chain, dragging him up the stairs to the truck, while Cole moves to the right.

We place the men in the bed of the truck, and the boys jump in behind to make sure they don't wake and try to jump out. They place a tarp over the bodies before they get comfortable, seated in the bed. I get in the driver's seat and head toward the club. We pull up to the back, where I put the truck in park. The boys jump out of the bed, dragging the men out. I open the back door, holding it open for them to come through.

We head down to the basement, taking the steps two at a time. Turning on the lights, I head over to the sink and grab two buckets. I add ice and water to each. As I'm prepping the buckets, chains rattle as Cole and Cade lift the slouched bodies. They connect them to the hooks hanging from the ceiling, pulling the chain link down to place the men on their knees. I throw a bucket of ice water over each of them, watching as they gasp for air. Watching every move of their bodies, I circle them like I'm hunting my prey.

"Tell me, did you enjoy your nap? Are you ready to give me the answers I need or die like cowards?"

"We aren't telling you filthy Wolves shit, so scamper away with your tails tucked between your legs." Seems like he is going to be the fun one. I smile, throwing my head back, and howl. Without warning, I slam my fist into his jaw. His head snaps to the side, mouth already bleeding from the impact.

"Try again." I look over at the other and prowl toward him. "Who do you work for, and why are you in my town?" He stares ahead, not saying a word. I connect my fist to his face. The beating continues between myself and the boys for another hour, with their blood on my jacket and hands.

I crouch to their level. The tough guy throws his head back, and before I can react, he headbutts me right in the face, causing my mask to dig into my face. I shoot up and kick him in his chest, causing him to slam into the wall behind him, hitting his head.

"Keep them chained up and see if you can get any answers out of them." I walk up the stairs, slamming the door. Yanking the mask off, blood runs down my face. I walk up to my office, going straight to my chair to grab the remote, turning the screen to the cameras in the basement. Walking over to the bar and grabbing a glass, I unscrew the cap to the whiskey bottle and pour myself a drink.

Sinking into the couch, I take a deep swig of the whiskey, savoring the burn as it goes down my throat. Why are they here, and what do they want? If they are part of the Snakes, they have become very bold, as they never stepped into our territory before. What changed? What is here that they decided to slither out of the shadows and play?

I observe the surveillance, watching as Cade and Cole take their turns on each of them. They're still not talking. I'll give it to them; they aren't going to break easily. I'll give them a couple of days chained up with no food to see if they go mad and we can get something out of them. My phone chimes, and I pull it out of my pocket to see who the text is from. Hoping it's Regan, I'm quickly disappointed.

The last time I had anything to do with Morgan was when I was still going through my trials. I have no idea what she wants or why she is reappearing, but I swore her off. She's walking drama, and I'm not getting tangled up in that again. The last thing I need is for her to get in between me and Regan. I can tell Regan is starting to let down her barrier to me. Whether I am forcing it down little by little or she likes the games we are playing, she is going to break any moment.

I scroll to Morgan's contact, and I push block. Maybe she will leave me alone now that she can't reach me. Looking at the time, I see that it's already 4:30 a.m. I really need to get back home and take a hot shower. My muscles ache and I could use some sleep.

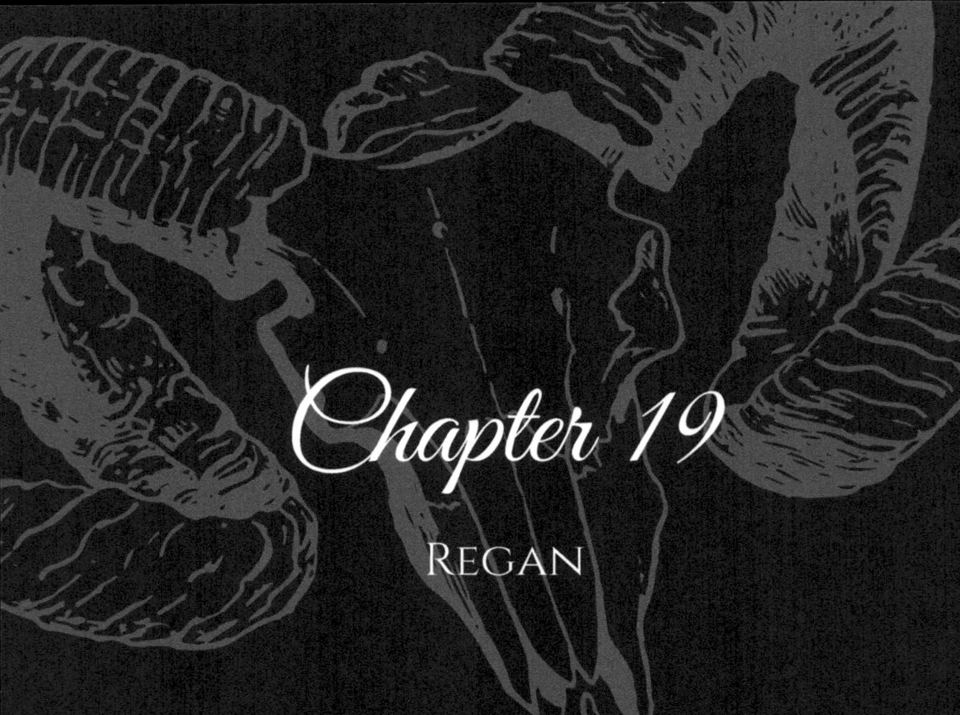

Chapter 19

REGAN

After my shift, Seth brought me home, stopping in the parking garage and letting my oh so mighty bodyguards tail me into the elevator.

It happened again. I couldn't say no when my body screamed yes. A part of me thinks I should just give in to him. I was in love with him once. Maybe after I left, he realized he royally fucked up. He is the only person I have ever felt safe with, but also terrified of, at the same time. Maybe he can protect me from HIM.

Maybe if HE sees that I am under Seth's protection, he won't come after me. I would rather die than be back under his control.

After my shower, I pop some popcorn, grab a Dr. Pepper, and head over to the couch. I flip through the TV and find

Practical Magic, one of my favorite movies. Must've dozed off because I wake up to the ding of the elevator. I look at the clock on the wall and see it's almost five a.m. Seth walks through the entrance with blood stained on his face and hands. He looks exhausted.

Jumping up from the couch, heart racing at the sight of him, I rush over to where he freezes in place. "Seth, what the fuck happened? Are you hurt? Are you okay?" I grab his arm, walking over to the stool and pushing him to sit. Hurrying over to the sink, I grab a rag, running it under warm water. I stride over to him, cupping his face as he stays silent, watching me. Gently cleaning his face, getting rid of the blood, I notice a deep gash at his temple. I grab the first aid kit from under the sink to clean it up.

"Seth, what happened?" I try again to see if he will answer me. I knew he was powerful, and I knew he didn't take shit from anyone, but I've never seen him in this state.

"Nothing, just business I had to take care of." He sighs, pushing off the stool to head to his bedroom.

"Are you really part of the Wolves? Please, give me something," I ask, changing up my question and following him.

"It's late, Regan; I need a shower. Yes, I'm part of the Wolves. I thought you knew that, considering who our parents are. Now go to sleep." He walks away, closing the door to his room. I stand there for a minute, trying to sort out my thoughts. Seeing him like that scared me. Not scared of him, but scared I will lose him. Call me crazy, because I definitely am, but I can't help this feeling of wanting to give in even more.

I hear the shower turn on, showing me that he really is done with this conversation. Today has been a long day. I turn and head into my room. Shutting the door, I climb into bed. I snuggle under the blankets and quickly fall into a deep sleep.

I wake up to the bed dipping and the comforter moving. I stay very still, keeping my eyes shut. His spice scented body wash surrounds me, and his arm wraps around my waist, snuggling up next to me. I let go of the breath I didn't know I was holding. I am instantly warm and protected. Can't he always be like this? Maybe then I wouldn't want to hate him and also be with him at the same time.

I don't shove him away; I let him stay there. Maybe he needed some peace after whatever he was dealing with tonight.

It's been a week since the night he first came into my room. The club has been closed due to some construction, per Seth. I've spent my days hanging out with Alex, using the building's gym, and binge-watching shows on TV. There is a new coffee shop that just opened across the street. I'm dying for some good coffee and to see if they have any treats.

I hop up from the couch and head to my room, getting changed quickly. I sling over my cross-body purse and slide on my Vans. The elevator doors open to take me to the lobby right above the garage. I step in and pop in my headphones. The elevator gets to the bottom and opens up to the bodyguards positioned at the bottom. You would think I would already be used to them, but I shake my head and roll my eyes. I can feel them following me from behind. I hear my phone ding, and I dig it out.

Seth: Where are you heading, my little spawn?
Thinking of running?
Took you long enough.

Me: I didn't know I had to check in any time I left, considering I have these two puppets following me around.

Seth: I could always string you up on a leash and make you my puppet.

Me: *Sends him the middle finger emoji*
I'm only headed to the new coffee shop across the street, need one?

Seth: Aww, is the spawn being sweet?
No, I'm good. In a meeting,
will be home in a couple hours.

I pocket my phone and head across the street. I order a caramel macchiato and a scone, then sit at a table outside. It's so nice outside this time of year, and with Mardi Gras coming up, there are decorations filling the door frames and streets—people laughing and loud music playing. I can smell the gumbo cooking, preparing for the festivities later on. Maybe I'll check it out and dance in the streets with Alex.

I sit there for a little while, finishing up the last of my coffee. I get up to throw away my trash and head back down the block to go to a cute herb shop to grab some natural teas for the penthouse. The shop smells amazing, like lavender and spices. The shopkeeper is so adorable, with her white hair in a tight bun on the top of her head and bangles lining her arms. She smiles up at me, asking if I needed help, and I tell her I am just looking around. I find a couple of jars and pay.

I walk out of the shop and a little boy almost bumps into me. "Are you Regan?" Confused, I nod my head. "This is for you. A man asked me to give it to you." He hands me a bag and runs off. I see a note on the bag, and curious, I unfold it.

Little dove, you can run, but you can't hide.

I start to shake and I open the bag to find three dead crows. I'm not very superstitious, but I know dead crows mean that death is coming. A scream bursts out of my mouth, dropping the bag. I back up, shaking my head. This can't be happening. I think I hear horns blaring, but my ears are ringing so loud that I'm not really sure.

"Ma'am, watch out!" I feel instant pain on my side, and suddenly I'm flying. I land on the roof of a car, and I hit the street. Through my squinted eyes, I see the car take off. I can't breathe. My body is shaking. I feel pain shooting up everywhere, then hands are on me, checking to see if I still have a pulse. I can't move; I can't speak. I hear people crowding, someone calling 911.

I feel hands on my neck, holding it for support—sirens blaring and coming to a stop. People rushing toward me with what sounds like a gurney.

"Keep supporting her head so we can place a brace on and transfer her to the gurney." I hear another male voice next to me. I try to speak; I try to ask what happened. But nothing comes out. Is this what it feels like when you die? Wordless, out of control?

I'm moving and the person walking with me is on the phone. Yelling into it, "Pick up. Pick up, pick up."

Then everything goes black, and I float into nothingness.

Chapter 20

Seth

Getting home last night, I didn't expect Regan to react the way she did. I should've showered at the club to avoid her seeing me like that. I shouldn't make her worry the way that I did, but I also don't regret it because I got to see a spark of emotion and care from her, like we were when we were younger. It felt good being taken care of for once. The way she looked at me, the way she cleaned me up, sparked something in me—something I didn't know I could feel.

Without a word, I disappear into my room, leaving her in the living room, standing there alone. I wasn't ready to give her the answers she wanted. My business was not her burden to bear. After I showered, I got dressed and went to her room. I didn't know why my feet carried me that way. But when I saw her sleeping peacefully in her bed, I wanted to wrap my arms around her and hold her. I wanted to take her scent in and devour any source of peace she offered. I soon fell into a deep sleep, like I was home.

It's been a week since I had snuck into her bed and held her. A part of me wanted to just move her to my room and never let her leave. And now, I'm sitting in my office at the club, completing paperwork that needs catching up on and watching surveillance to see if I can get any hints on who is behind Regan's threat and interference with the Wolves' shipments. I observe some hooded men around the shipment warehouse, but then the feed cuts and I can never catch their faces.

My phone dings and I pick it up, noticing that Regan left the building. What is she up to? I sure as shit hope she is not stupid enough to make a run for it. I mean, this past week, we have been getting along better, besides her throwing a fit that her Dr. Pepper had disappeared, thanks to Cole, and the eye rolls when the boys are over.

Me: Where are you heading, my little spawn?
Thinking of running?
Took you long enough.

Regan: I didn't know I had to check in any time I left, considering I have these two puppets following me around.

I can't help the smirk and chuckle that rumbles my chest to her feisty little remark. Thinking of the scowl she probably has on her face makes me want to wipe that attitude right off her face and remind her of who she belongs to.

Me: I could always string you up on a leash and make you my puppet.

Regan: *Sends him the middle finger emoji * I'm only headed to the new coffee shop across the street, need one?

Me: Aww, is the spawn being sweet? No, I'm good. In a meeting, will be home in a couple hours.

Right when I set my phone back on the table, it starts to ring. Seeing my father's picture on the screen, I answer the phone, knowing it may be some more intel about the two fuckers in the basement.

"Have you been able to get anything out of the two you have in custody?" Well, hi to you, too. Always serious and never 'how are you?'

"They haven't said anything yet. They were trained well, but I've been reviewing the surveillance and noticed hooded men at the warehouse this morning. Then the screen went out. Do we have any Wolves over there today?" I ask, wondering if it was some sort of initiation or training they have the new Wolves doing.

My father goes silent for a minute. "We only have the workers there that are taking care of the shipment and some guards. We need to get over there now." He hangs up the phone before I can even respond. Fuck! I jump out of my seat and call Cole to get his ass to the warehouse as I am sprinting out of the club.

We get to the warehouse, and it's ghostly quiet. We normally are greeted by someone, and there is usually activity going in and out. I pull on my hood and place my mask on my face. Looking at Cole, we pull our guns out and walk slowly toward the building. We press our backs to the side of the door before sneaking through. Creeping inside, pointing my gun, I get hit with a rotting flesh smell. We can't see shit and I almost lose my footing to a slippery substance on the floor.

We find the breaker and reset the lights. What the fuck? Hanging from every piece of equipment are bodies, corpses are hung by their necks, their chests cut open. Bodies are spread across the floors, with blood soaking the concrete.

"What kind of sick fuck does this? How the fuck were they able to destroy this many people?" Cole is covering his mouth, trying not to vomit.

There are crows picking at the bodies, like they were brought in here on purpose. There is no way in hell they could have gotten in with the doors shut. I round a corner, and on the wall is another body hanging, with a wolf mask on their face. Next to the body, the wall has been smeared with a message in blood.

The Empire will fall. It is time the Wolves learn their place. Every single drop of your blood will taste sweeter when you are eliminated one by one.

I hear cars pulling up on the gravel and men sprinting toward the building. As the men pile in and the Elders step through the doors, everyone freezes. I quickly take a picture of the message on the wall. What the fuck happened for them to rebel against us to this extent?

"War has officially been brought to our door. We need to kill every fucking Snake that slithers in our streets. Find them, kill them, and deliver them to their doorstep. Seth, I need you to push harder on the two you have. Anyone who resembles higher power, bring them to the club. We will not rest until the trash is disposed of." I look over at the Elder who is talking. Regan's father has fire blazing in his eyes. He comes to stand next to me, eyeing the message.

"Get this shit cleaned up. We do not say a word to anyone if they weren't here. We don't need them knowing that they got under our skin. They will soon know who runs this town and who will take over their territory and make them bend to their knees as we burn them alive." He walks out of the building.

I nod at the men surrounding us, and they start to grab bodies, getting the crows out of the warehouse, and scatter to find anything useful.

I head to the warehouse office to check the closed-circuit surveillance. Entering the office, I pull my hood down, take off the mask, and I click through the camera footage. There are time lapses missing, as if hours went by, but no movement. That's not normal, especially for how busy the warehouse is. There's no way a mass murder occurs with no trace of life. Hacking into data, I enter a series of codes. The screen blurs with numbers, letters, and symbols becoming one. Finally, after twenty minutes of coding, I break through the wall and the missing clips pop up, one by one. We stand there frozen in anticipation as the first clip comes to life.

The intruders are hooded, shielding their identities from our sight. Gunshots are fired. Our boys put up one hell of a fight, but there were too many of them. I notice a couple of the hooded men sustained only superficial gunshot wounds, and they had hurried out of the building. There has to be a hint. I need to keep an eye out to see if I can find any men on the streets that need to be picked up and brought to me.

"What in the fuck? Do we have any idea what they're after? Why strike now? And what's their motive?" Cole is leaning over my shoulder, watching the video from behind.

"I have no idea, but we need to figure out how they got access without being detected. How did they know where our cameras are located? We need to hammer down who the rat is within our Empire." Rewinding the videos, trying to catch any glimpse of who the rat is or if they were present.

My phone rings, and I pull it out to see who it is—Cade. I don't have time for anything else right now. Hitting decline, I shove my phone back in my pocket. I run my hand through my hair; it's going to be a long night. We sit here scrolling through the footage over and over again, trying to find something. I stop on a clip that shows a hooded shadow with their head down, sitting at the warehouse door, leaning against it while the chaos takes place.

I try to zoom in, but can't get a visual of the face. What I do notice is that the sleeves are pushed up, and a skull tattoo with a snake wrapped around it and another tattoo that I can't seem to place are visible.

"Cole, I think I found something. This male right here, this tattoo, it looks familiar, but I can't place it, can't make out the second tattoo." I point at the screen.

"That's the Snakes' tattoo, which confirms the Elders' suspicion. I have seen it on one of the prisoners in the basement. We can head over there and see if we can get more answers." He rubs his hand on his face.

My phone rings again, but I ignore it. We're onto something. I can't get distracted. My phone vibrates with an incoming text. I pull out my phone and see it is Cade again.

My heart stops and my face goes white. No. No. No. This can't be happening.

Chapter 21

SETH

I'm racing through town with Cole in the passenger seat on the phone with Alex. Alex is already at the hospital with Regan, giving him updates. Cade contacted her, trying to find us. My mind is racing, and I can't hear anything other than the ringing in my ears. I didn't protect her. What if they got to her? Where the fuck were the guards assigned to watch over her? These cars need to get the fuck out of my way.

I come to a screeching halt at the hospital entrance and bolt out of the truck. I can hear someone yelling at me that I can't leave my truck there. To hell with them. I get to the desk, asking for Regan's room.

"I'm sorry, sir—family only at this time, but you can wait in the waiting room." She motions to the other side of the desk.

"You got me fucked up if you think that I'm staying in the waiting room when my woman is up there." Red blurs my vision. I could fucking hit her. Fully aware she is just doing her job, but I need to get to Regan to see how bad it is. I can't help but feel responsible. This is all my fault. I should have protected her better.

"I'm sorry, sir. If you're not married, you are not going back at this time until we have approval." Cole grabs my arm, pulling me to the side. He is trying to keep me from making a bigger scene, but if Alex were in this position, he would burst through the doors and turn this place upside down—which I am about to do.

"Seth, keep it cool. You have the look in your eye like you're going to slit her throat. We'll get back there; I'll make some phone calls and..." A buzzer goes off and the door opens. For a second, I think about sprinting through the door, but a doctor and Regan's father walk out, doing a double take when he sees me.

"Kingsley, what are you doing standing out here? I see now where all the noise is coming from." He turns to the nurse, shooting her daggers. "Why haven't you let him in? You do realize he's a Kingsley? His father and I fund this hospital. If you knew what was good for you and your job, you would have let him through."

The admin's face goes pale, tears welling in her eyes. "I-I'm sorry, sir. I didn't know. P-Please go in. She is in room 205." I walk past her desk toward the door. Stopping for a second and nodding at Regan's father, he claps my back. I rush through the halls, trying to find her room. My heart's racing. Please, please be okay. I round the corner and see the room and swing open the door. Alex jumps to her feet, eyes wide, and puts her finger over her mouth, signaling me to keep quiet.

I look over at Regan. Her eyes are closed, but she's breathing steadily. She has bruises and cuts on her arms, bandages on her forehead, and wires hooked up to her arms and chest. She's breathing, meaning she's alive. There's a slight ease to how I feel, but how bad is it? I stand and stare at her, my body frozen in place. A hand is placed on my back, and I flinch. I break my stare and look over at Alex.

"She's okay, Seth. There's a couple of broken ribs—nothing punctured—a gash on her head, and she has a concussion. She's been sleeping for a while, hasn't woken up since I've been here, but the doctor said it is a miracle she had only minor injuries. Go sit with her; I'll leave you with her." Giving me a little shove toward the chair next to the bed, she makes her way out of the room.

I lean over Regan, brushing my fingertips down the side of her face. I kiss her forehead and sit down in the chair, lacing my fingers through hers. Before I knew it, I'm waking up to the sounds of movement from her, and my eyelids fly open. Looking over at the clock, it's been hours. I look back at her and her eyes slowly open. She scrunches her face and goes to sit up, but winces. I push her shoulder back lightly to guide her back down.

"Easy, love. You need to lie back down. You're safe, I promise." I keep my voice low, trying to be soothing.

"How long have I been here? I should've stayed at the penthouse and listened to you. I just wanted coffee. You don't have to stay; I'm not your problem." Shaking her head, she's trembling. Why would she think she is a problem?

"Regan, look at me." Her glossy eyes meet mine. I cup her face in my hands and kiss her softly. "You are not a problem to me. Don't ever say that again. I didn't protect you. I wasn't there. I failed you, but I promise you that I'll burn this damn city down before I let any more harm come your way."

Tears roll down her face. "Seth, you hate me. Why would you give two shits about what happens to me? You proved that years ago. I don't understand any of this. Plus, this is my fault. I stepped right off the curb in the way of the car." She sniffs, shifting to the other side of the bed, like she's trying to get away from me.

Pain shoots through me. I can't take this. I can't leave her thinking I hate her, that I'm using her, or even pitying her. "I have never hated you. I've wanted you to be mine since we were kids. We danced around each other, but once I came of age to join the Wolves, it was my fate, not yours. I didn't want you to be involved in this world more than you already were with your father being an Elder. I knew I was not good for you. You left, and although it pained me to see you leave, I knew it was the best thing for you. You came back, and I couldn't stay away from you. This time, you are mine. I'm not letting you go again."

I let it out. God, I feel like a pussy, spilling my feelings. But she had to know. I couldn't watch her move away from me like that. I may be a monster, but I will never hurt her again. She doesn't say a word. She stares at me, trying to read my face, my body language—trying to figure out if I'm lying. I don't expect her to say anything. I don't need her to. I will prove it to her, prove that I'm the only man she needs, wants, and trusts.

A couple of hours go by, nurses and doctors coming in and out to check vitals and give Regan medication for pain. We haven't said much to each other, but the silence is comforting. The doctor advised that if everything remains stable, then she can go home tomorrow. We sit and watch reruns of SVU, and I check with the boys to get updates on the warehouse to see if they came upon any new leads.

I keep thinking about what Regan told me about tripping and getting hit. She's not clumsy. Things are not adding up. I send a quick text to Cade to see if he can find any video surveillance from the area where she was hit to see if it was really a trip or if something bigger happened and if she is keeping something from me. She looked terrified as she told me, like she was scared to speak up, and that is not her. She has a mouth that could make a grown man cry. Something is up, and I don't understand why she wouldn't just tell me the truth. Well, maybe I do. She doesn't trust or believe me yet.

I recall when I first arrived and couldn't get in. If it wasn't for her father, I'm not sure if I would have been able to get back here without using my title, which I would have. A thought crosses my mind, and I smirk. There is one way I can ensure her safety and not have this issue again. She will never agree, but it is what's best for her. I pull out my phone and send a text to Alex to come back to the room so I can step out. I also send a text to Cole to come back with her to keep an eye on the girls. The admin won't fuss at this point, after Regan's father made threats.

Me: Father, Dale, can you both meet me in 20 minutes at the church and bring Judge Anders along?.

Father: Did something happen? Do you have an update on the warehouse? Is Regan okay?

Me: No updates at this time, but Regan is fine. I have a favor to ask, and it is better to speak in person.

Dale: We will meet you at the church.

I slide my phone into my pocket and stand just as Cole and Alex walk in. "I'll be back in an hour. I have to take care of something important. Call me and I can be back sooner." I lean over to kiss Regan's forehead and head out of the room before I get bombarded by questions I can't answer right now.

Twenty minutes later, pulling up to the church, I notice that my father and Dale are already here. Getting out of the truck and taking a deep breath, I hope they agree, so this process will be smoother and easier. Shutting my door, I head into the church. They come into view, and I notice Judge Anders is here already, too. Perfect. They watch me step into the church, and I nod at them, taking a spot at the table they are sitting at.

"Son, what is so urgent?" My father looks at me, observing my body language. "Out with it, boy; we don't have all day."

"I need your blessing and paperwork drawn up and delivered to me before tomorrow. I have chosen whom I'm going to marry. This would be the best choice for her." I look over at Dale. "I want your blessing to marry Regan. This would ensure her safety, unite our families, and our history makes sense for us to marry."

All three men stare at me, expressionless. I am only asking for their blessing to show respect and so they can help me get papers drawn now and in secret. Even if they don't agree, I will find another way.

Dale is the first to speak. "What makes you think she will agree? Her stubborn ass hardly listens to me, as an Elder or her father."

"She will not be aware we are married until after the papers are signed. I'll slip the papers under her discharge documents, and she'll sign without knowing. I will tell her soon, but after what happened at the warehouse and then her incident, this is how I can keep her safe, marked as an ol' lady. Once things calm down, I'll tell her what I did. I might get stabbed, but she will just have to understand." I look between my father and Dale. Come on, come on. This would be the best scenario for both of them. Two powerful houses united as one, the family would be untouchable. I assume they are thinking the same thing when they look at each other and nod.

"Anders, get the paperwork over to the hospital. Seth will have them signed and back to you tomorrow. You are to process them within 24 hours of obtaining them." Father turns to Anders.

Anders doesn't look shocked at this request. He has been quiet this whole time, observing. He has always done my father's bidding without a single question. Loyalty runs deep between the three. My father and Dale—Elders who are never questioned—and Anders, who is a Wolf and also a judge. He controls the justice system to keep the Wolves out of the spotlight.

Nodding his head, "I'll head to the office now and get the papers drawn up. Give me thirty minutes and I'll have them ready for you. Swing by before you go back to the hospital. I will meet you at the hospital tomorrow to collect the signed documents and have them processed. Congratulations are in order." Getting up from the table, he claps me on the back and heads out the door.

"Boy, you better be ready for war once you tell her. She will drag you to Hell and back. I suggest you keep your distance when you break the news." Dale gets up from the table with a smile on his face, shaking his head.

I would love to see my little spawn drag me to Hell. I would gladly get on my knees and crawl behind her as long as she goes with me.

Chapter 22

REGAN

Waking up to Seth sitting next to me in the hospital took me by surprise. I wasn't expecting him to be here, with a worried look on his face. I knew he would hear about it, but didn't think he would actually care. We had gone around in circles, growing up, and then he dismissed me like I was some sort of trash on the side of the road. His forcing me to live with him seemed more of a power trip than anything. It was like he had to show he was in charge and held all the power.

He had spilled the truth that he had done what he did years ago, because of actually his feelings for me. This man, with his scary as hell, don't give a fuck, attitude, and who most likely does terrifying things, got soft with me. Part of me wanted to believe it was just a ploy, a pity, but the other part of me wanted to give in and melt. I didn't respond to his confession because, quite frankly, I don't know how to take it.

How can I still hate a man who will go to the end of the world to make sure I'm safe, even when I feel like a prisoner? He has secrets; he has the Empire; he has this fire that makes grown men cry and shit themselves. He has a dominance that I love to challenge and test the boundaries of, but Seth Kingsley would never hurt me, even if he hated my guts. When he left the hospital to take care of business, I caught myself daydreaming of what life would be like with him: chaos, fighting for dominance, testing each other's limits.

My mind flutters to thoughts of him touching me—rough, but soft. He would be painful, but still make my knees go weak. He lights a fire in me that begs him to do dirty things: tie me up, demand that I beg for him, and make me ache until I can't take it anymore. My mind drifts to the masked Wolf who had kidnapped me and fucked me. I loved it. I wanted more, just thinking about it makes me wet.

Does it make me sick in the head? Considering my past and the shit done to me, I would never want that to happen again. But this was different; he wasn't hurting me. Is it because it was two different people taking away my freedom at that moment? Who was this masked wolf? Would Seth give me what I wanted?

"Hello, earth to Regan. Are you okay? Do I need to call the doctor to check on you?" Alex takes my shoulders into her hands and gives me a little shake. While my mind has been wandering, apparently Alex has been talking to me this whole time.

"No, I'm fine. Sorry, I had other things on my mind. Does anyone know where Seth went, anyway?" Looking over, I can see the concern in her eyes. Maybe I'm going crazy, with the look she is giving me.

"He didn't say where he was going, but said he would be back soon. You know, he freaked out in the lobby when they wouldn't let him back here. What is going on between you two, anyhow? You didn't kick him out like you normally would."

"How do you know he freaked out? Honestly, I have no idea. One minute he is snarky, giving me the evil eye, and the next, he walks in here like he gives a shit. He told me things that my brain can't comprehend. Do I believe him? My brain is screaming no, but after seeing him worried about me, I do. Do I trust him? Not quite. I'm worried I'm going to be tossed to the side again." Taking a shuddering breath, I tilt my head back to stare at the ceiling. Do I want to believe him? My heart is saying yes, he will protect you and there will always be lingering feelings, but my brain is telling me to stay the fuck away before I get crushed again.

"I was not there when he flipped out, but Cole told me." Snapping out of my thoughts, I look back at Alex. Her face softens as she talks about him to me. "Being part of the Empire is weird. You are taught to be one way, almost like a robot. He will go to the end of the depths for you. Being with someone like them is not easy. They come and go, and you are not to ask why or where they go. You have to take their baggage and anger at times, but at the end of the day, I am protected and wanted, and I would never trade it. Seth is not only protecting you, but himself. What he did in the past, I don't agree with, but I am sure he has his reasons." Taking my hand in one of hers and brushing my hair with the other, she kisses my forehead.

"You are my best friend, and if I thought you weren't safe with him or I didn't trust him, I would tell you to turn your happy ass back to school. But fate works in weird ways, and bringing you back together should mean something. Give it a shot, or don't, that's up to you."

"Thank you, Alex. He lights a fire in me. Even when I'm being an ass and trying to push back and stay away from him, my mind wanders back to him. Seeing him after so many years has triggered so many feelings. I loved him, but he kicked me to the curb. Ughhh. I feel crazy."

We sit silent for a few minutes. It is nice to not say a word, but my best friend understands me. She knows me better than anyone in this world, and taking her advice might be what I need: give him a chance, but keep my guard up.

Ten minutes later, Seth comes back into the room with Cole. He's looking like he just won the lottery. Not to mention that he looks like a million bucks. God, what the hell are you doing to me?

Eyeing me like he is inspecting for any new signs of injuries, he asks, "How are you feeling, little spawn?"

"Like I got hit by a car." I chuckle, causing shooting pain in my ribs. In a blink of an eye, he is by my side, asking what I need, where I hurt, and if I need the doctor. "Seth, I'm fine. I'm alive, just don't make me laugh. My ribs hurt," I say, trying to hold in another laugh. What is happening to me? I'm all giddy, like I'm back in high school.

"That's not funny, Regan, you could've been killed. The doctor said you can be released tomorrow, and I will take you back to the penthouse, where you can rest comfortably. The club is still closed, so you don't have to worry about work. I don't want you leaving the penthouse without me." His eyes darken with a possessive look. I just nod my head in agreement.

It's mid-afternoon the next day, and per the doctor, everything is looking good—besides the broken ribs and banged up head—but they don't see a problem with releasing me. They advise me to take it easy for healing, and if I have any blackouts or concerns with my concussion, to come back immediately.

Part of me is relieved to go home, but I keep thinking about the package I got. I know he has found me. How am I supposed to stay safe? Do I tell Seth about HIM and what I ran away from? My anxiety sets off. I take deep breaths to calm down before Seth comes back in. I'm just not ready to talk about my past.

Seth walks back in with paperwork from the doctor, walking over to me and sitting in the chair that has been there all night, with him never leaving my side. He looks exhausted. I told him to go home and get rest, that I would be fine, but his stubborn ass wouldn't leave.

I sign the papers as he directs, not bothering to read them, as I am sure he already did that for me. He walks back out to turn the paperwork in to the doctor, and my mind wanders to if things are going to change once we get home. Home. What a strange thing to think, as I was forced to live with him against my will.

I push up onto my elbows, moving my body to the edge of the bed to get out of this hideous hospital gown, when Seth walks in and rushes over to me.

"What do you think you're doing? You're going to hurt yourself. Stay still." He pushes my shoulders down and walks over to retrieve my clothes.

"Seth, I'm not dying and I'm not broken. I can get my clothes on myself. I'm a grown ass woman and don't need someone babysitting and dressing me 24/7." Rolling my eyes, I start to stand, but quickly sit back down, wincing at the pain from my ribs.

He walks back over to me with a smirk on his damn face. "What was that you were saying, love? I think I caught you wincing as you were trying to disobey the big bad wolf." He unties my gown from the back. Oh, god, he's going to see me fully naked.

His eyes travel along my body as he brings my bra up to put on me, but stops mid air. He brushes his hand right under my breast and notices the scar where I was cut by HIM. He then travels down to my left hip, where another scar is. FUCK. His eyes darken, eyebrows creased in. "Where did you get these? How did you get these?"

"It was an accident when I was away. Don't worry about it." Grabbing my bra and putting my arms through, I try to clasp it, wincing and struggling to get the damn thing on. He hovers over me, taking over clasping my bra, and helps me with my shirt. Grabbing my elbow, he lifts me to a standing position, sliding my thong slowly up my legs. His fingers' feather-like touches up my thigh make my breath hitch.

His finger then touches my folds as he glides my thong straps to my waist. He knows exactly what he is doing, and I know that because he has a stupid ass smirk on his face again. He pulls on my shorts, buttoning me up. He grabs my socks and shoes, putting them on.

He leans over me again, looking into my eyes, his lips coming to my ear, his breath causes me to shiver again. "Only good girls get rewarded." Jesus, just send me to hell because him dressing me, touching me, breathing in my ear, and those words, should not make me wet. More like soaked.

Chapter 23

Seth

I enjoy seeing her squirm. My touch affects her, just as she affects me with a single look. After getting her dressed, regardless of trying to be independent, she clings to me as I lift her in my arms, placing her into a wheelchair. I send a quick text to Cade that we're headed outside so he can pull the truck around. We head to the front of the hospital silently. I keep going back to those scars on her body. I don't remember seeing those when I had her chained to the table. Those scars, hidden, full of secrets. Those scars don't look like they were an accident. There has to be a story, and if she doesn't tell me, I will figure it out on my own.

The doors to the front slide open and we walk out, the breeze sending goosebumps down Regan's arms. She instinctively crosses her arms, rubbing her hands up and down them. Cade pulls the truck up, and I stop the wheelchair, locking the wheels. Walking over to the passenger side, I open up the door, grab her arm lightly, then help her up and lift her into the seat. I take the seat belt and she swats me away, but I ignore her and buckle her in.

Cade already has the wheelchair back to the doors and hops into the back seat. I jump into the driver's seat and pull out of the hospital. I switch on the radio, because the silence is heavy, and it's driving me insane. Bad Omens start to play, calming me down.

"Nice seeing you're alive and moving, Regan. Considering that when I found you, you looked fucked up." Cade leans against the back seat, draping his arms across the seat.

"Looks like nothing's changed and you still have to be a stuck up ass who can't just say hi." She rolls her eyes, crossing her arms over her chest. "Thanks for finding me and getting me help. How did you know where I was, anyway? I didn't see you around with the pack of stalkers Seth set up for me."

"All I'm saying is you don't look like death, and I'm glad you didn't die because that one over there would have killed us all." He chuckles and points to me. "I was headed back to the penthouse to check in and release one of your 'stalkers' when I heard a screeching and saw you flying through the air."

A couple of hand gestures sent back and forth, eye rolls, and name calling continue the whole way home. If I was a betting man, I would say they were related. We pull up to the penthouse, heading down into the garage. We come to a stop, and I'm instantly out of the truck, going to the passenger side. Helping her out, I go to pick her up and carry her to the elevator, but she swats me away, grumbling about how her legs still work. I let her walk, but stay close.

"I've got it from here, Cade. Thanks for the help. I'll meet up with you and Cole later; we have things to discuss." He nods at the both of us and heads to his truck. I catch Regan looking around the parking garage with worry in her eyes. I look around, trying to figure out what she is looking for, but she turns and quickens her step into the elevator. What is that about?

As we head into the elevator, the doors shutting, she looks relieved. "Are you doing okay? Is there something out there that has you spooked?" I move closer to her, grabbing her gently so I don't hurt her ribs, and bring her into me. At first, she is tense and tries to pull away, but she nestles her face into my side and relaxes.

"I'm okay. I think I am just tired and need to clean up, and get some rest. Getting hit like I did, it just makes a girl a little jumpy. I'm fine. I promise."

I wrap my other arm around her, like a protective barrier, and hold her. I brush her hair from her face and kiss her forehead. "You're lying, but I want you to know that I won't let anything happen to you. I will find out what is haunting you." The elevator door opens, and Regan pulls away from me, walking into the living room. Heading into her bedroom, she turns on her light.

I walk in after her and go into her bathroom, starting a hot bath with essential oils and bubbles. She walks in, eyebrows raised, and I gesture for her to come over, gently undressing her. I help her into the bath, and she winces as she lowers into the tub.

Tilting her head back, she closes her eyes. "Thank you for the bath, but I won't drown. There aren't any monsters in the tub. You can go do whatever you have to do with the boys."

Bending my knees on the side of the tub and leaning over, I grab the loofah. Pouring soap on it, I lift her arm and rub the loofah up and down. "I'm not going anywhere until you are clean. Can't have you missing any spots on this perfect body." I move the loofah across her chest and down her other arm. Her breathing picks up and my cock twitches. I look up and down her beautiful body and can't help but admire her beauty. Her body is covered in suds, dripping down her beautiful plumb breasts.

I move her to sit up, moving my fingers under her chin, tilting her head backward. Grabbing a pitcher, I pour water onto her hair until it is soaking. Lathering her hair with shampoo, she lets out a moan. Rinsing her hair, I then apply conditioner and repeat the process. After finishing, she leans back into the tub, and I cup water in my hands, rinsing her body of the suds, brushing against her body. I know she is wet, and not from the water in the tub.

Running my hands up her thighs, I feel her tense, but continue. She doesn't stop me. We lock eyes and I travel up and stop right before her pretty pussy. Going off her instincts, she opens her legs wider for me, and I take that as an invitation.

I rub my fingers on her clit in circles and plunge my middle finger into her sweet cunt. Another moan escapes, and I slide in another finger. Pumping my fingers in and out, she begins to rock her hips. Her body knows what it wants, and it is addicted to me. My dick grows harder. I know I shouldn't be doing this—she just got out of the hospital—but I can't stop. She is a drug that I will gladly take over and over again. I pull my fingers out of her and she whimpers.

I smirk. I have her right where I want her. "Don't worry, my little spawn, we aren't done. I'll be gentle with you this one and only time, considering the circumstances. But going forward, you are going to take it like a good girl." Before she can answer, I lift her out of the tub gently and head over to the bed. She's soaking wet from the bath and the juices coming out of her sweet cunt that I can't wait to devour. I lay her down on the bed, and she goes for a blanket to cover herself.

Leaning over her, I yank the blanket from her and throw it onto the ground. "I am not done with you. I want a taste. You will keep your eyes on me as I devour your sweet cunt. Never move your eyes from mine. Do you understand?" She nods at me quickly as I run my hands down her body again. I pull her to the edge of the bed. She props up on her forearms as I kneel, spreading her legs open wide.

Her sweet cunt is so beautiful, and she is soaked, ready to be tasted. I lean in to glide my tongue up her folds. Fuck, she tastes amazing. Sucking on her clit, I hear her moan and look up to see her eyes trained on me. I keep my eyes locked on hers as I suck harder, plunging a finger inside of her, thrusting in and out of her, hard.

She clenches the sheets in her fists, panting, but her eyes never leave mine. I pull my fingers out, with her sweet, sweet cum all over. I stick them in my mouth and don't leave one drop, pulling my fingers out of my mouth with a pop. Her legs are shaking, and I dip my head back in between her legs and plunge my tongue inside of her and begin to feast.

"Fuck, Seth, don't stop. I'm going to cum again," she's screams.

I stop and she whines. "I want you to come on my face. I want you to watch me drink every last drop of you. I want you to scream my name and tell me who you belong to. Do you understand me?" Her eyes are wide, her body trembling. I smack her pussy and she jumps.

"I understand, just get your fucking face back between my legs, or I'm going to cum without you." Fuck, if my dick wasn't hard before, it's so fucking hard now that it hurts. Smacking her pussy again, I dive right in. Sucking, licking, biting, and that's what does it because she screams my name and releases all over my face. I take it all.

I undo my belt and push my pants and boxers down, pull my shirt over my head. Standing between her legs, her eyes trail down to my hard cock and her eyes go wide. My piercing at the tip glistens, and her eyes stare in wonder. Hovering over her, I waste no time and slam my cock inside her tight pussy.

Oh fuck, she is so tight. I let out a moan, thrusting harder and harder inside of her. Her hands are at my back, digging her nails into it as she scratches down. "God, you take my cock so well. Such a good girl." Raising her leg to wrap around my waist, I pump harder and harder into her.

"Who do you belong to?" I growl at her. She doesn't answer, and I slap her ass hard, causing her to wince. "I said, 'Who do you belong to?'"

"Y-You. Seth Kingsley. I belong to Seth Kingsley," she screams as she hits her peak.

I look between us, watching as my cock goes in and out. She's screaming as I thrust my final thrusts, and we hit our climaxes within a few seconds of each other. "Shit, little spawn. You're creaming all over my cock. I can see it. Your sweet pussy knows who it belongs to." I pull out, and she goes limp into the bed. We are both breathing heavily. I look up and down her body and think how beautiful and perfect her body is. I hear soft snores and notice she is passed out.

Pulling up my jeans and buckling my belt, throwing my shirt back on, I head to the bathroom and get her a warm washcloth. Walking back into the room, I lean over her, cleaning up her soaking pussy, then pull the blankets over her body. She rolls to her side where her ribs aren't broken and snuggles into the pillow. She is going to be sore tomorrow, but it was worth it. I can get used to this little spawn bringing me to my knees every night.

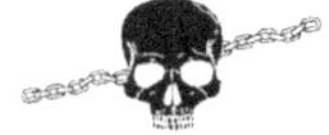

After making sure Regan is tucked in and safe in bed, I head to the elevator, heading down to the lobby where we have our own cigar bar. I walk through the doors to see that Cade and Cole are already sitting on the couches with glasses of whiskey in one hand and cigars in the other. Heading over to the bar, I order a drink and head over to where the boys are.

"There you are. Took you long enough to get your ass down here." Cole eyes me, slapping my back as I sit down.

"I had to make sure Regan was taken care of. What? Is Cade too boring and only I can pique your interest?" I chuckle to myself, taking a sip of my whiskey.

"Yeah, I bet you were taking care of her with the way you had a pep in your step walking in here." Cade eyes me like he heard us from all the way down here. Good. I hope everyone in this complex heard us and knows she is mine.

"Actually, I need you to do some digging for me. I have this feeling that this was not a freak accident. The way she was scanning the garage when we got home, she was terrified. She also has scars on her that she claims are from an accident, but they don't look that way. I need you to find surveillance from the shops she was at, so I can see what actually happened. I also need to know what happened when she was away. There is something more than what she is telling me. I need to know if the Snakes are involved, trying to attack me, or if there is something more." The boys nod their heads, pulling out their phones.

"I'll get with my connections and get ahold of the footage. While I wait for the footage, I'll also question some of the shop owners. As soon as I have the information, I'll send you a text and bring it to the club." Cade pockets his phone, taking another sip of his whiskey.

"I'll check in with Alex and see if there's anything she knows, since she is Regan's best friend, and make some calls to her college and see what I can find out." Cole drapes his arms across the back of the couch.

We sit there for a little longer, sipping our whiskey and smoking cigars. After we are done, I depart back to the penthouse, where the lights are dim, blackout curtains shut across the windows, and head to my room to shower. Standing under the steaming hot water, feeling my body relax, I lean my head forward and close my eyes.

Thinking back to our interaction earlier makes me smile. She may not know it, but she owns me. Every part of me. Should probably tell her what I have done, but things are starting to get good, and I don't want to start a war with my little demon just yet. Lathering up my body until every inch of me is clean, I rinse, shut the water off, and step out. Drying myself off, I slide my boxers on and head to my bed, but stop before I climb in. I head back to Regan's room and slide into her bed, draping my arm around her as she snuggles up against me. Taking in her sweet lavender scent, I drift into deep, peaceful sleep.

Chapter 24

Regan

It's been two weeks since I left the hospital, two weeks since I let Seth cross that dangerous line and liked it, two weeks since I let my walls down and feelings began to brew again. I may be an idiot, but I feel safe. I feel alive again. Hopefully, he doesn't run for the hills again and we can just be. My ribs have been healing great, the gash on my head is finally gone. It's been really quiet, with no threats coming my way. Maybe that's because I've been held up in the penthouse, not leaving except to go to doctor checkups, to which Seth took me.

Seth has been surprisingly nice, but I can also see his wheels turning, trying to figure out what happened that day. I know he doesn't believe me, but I'm just not ready to open that can of worms yet. I know that if I tell him what really happened with the accident, I'll have to unleash my past, and I don't know how he will react. Will he think that I'm a whore? That I let the shit happen? That I am just a weak little girl, and not good enough for him? I shake my head, stopping myself from going down that road.

Seth is at the club, taking care of some business with Cole and Cade. He made sure there were guards stationed for my safety. It's nice, but means I can't go anywhere without being stalked. I really hope the club gets back up and running soon because I'm ready to hear the bass dropping, the laughter, the drinks, and the tips! I am so bored in this damn house.

Walking out of my room, I head into the kitchen, opening up the fridge and grabbing myself a Dr. Pepper. I crack it open and take a deep swig, feeling the bubbles go down my throat. This, this is my drug. I could live off this bubbly goodness for the rest of my life! No one can tell me otherwise!

A light catches my eye in Seth's room. I know he's not home, so maybe he left a light on. Stepping into his room, I get hit with the smell of him, and shit, does it melt me to pieces. The light is coming from behind a large mirror that looks like a door that is slightly opened. Hmmm, that's weird. I never knew that was an actual door. Curiosity piques my interest, and I stand in front of the mirror, pulling it open wider. Part of me says not to go in there, that I am invading Seth's privacy and he will be pissed if I did, but the other part of me says to hell with it and to take a peek.

So, I let the devil on my right shoulder talk me into it and I go into the room. The walls are stone feeling and the floors are cement. It's a little chilly in here. I head toward the light at the end of the hall. There is another door where the light is shining, and I go to pull the handle. It's unlocked. I pause for a second before I open the door. Do I even want to know what is in this room? Absolutely. But do I want to get caught snooping? No. If I make it quick, he will never know.

Pulling the door open, it's lit up in a red glow. I walk further into the room and notice a table with chains, another counter that has a blindfold, knife, ball gag, and other items. Why the hell does this room look and feel familiar? I look up on the shelf and notice a wolf mask and gloves. I have been in here... realization hits me. No, it can't be. He can't be. No wonder I fucking liked it, as I feared for my life.

I hear the door squeak from behind me, and I spin around, jumping out of my skin. "You have been busy, my little spawn. Like what you see?" Seth growls, eyes narrowing on me as he slowly walks toward me. I back up and my ass hits the table.

"S-Seth..." I stutter, as my breathing picks up. He walks toward the table, touching the items. "It was you. You were the one who took me from the alley. You were the one who kidnapped me and brought me here, taking advantage of me." My body trembles as the event hits me harder.

"Took you long enough to figure it out. From what I remember, you enjoyed it. A lot, actually. My touch was familiar, made your sweet cunt wet. The first time I tasted you, I knew it wouldn't be the last. You are a drug that I won't let escape," he purrs as he takes two long strides, and he is instantly in front of me. "Care to experience it again? I'll give you a choice. Do you want to be blindfolded again, or would you like to see with your own eyes how terrified and good I can make you feel?"

I clench my legs together as my panties become soaked. I should be mad right now. No, I should be furious, but I'm not. All I want is to be his good girl and take it all. He brings his index finger to my chin and lefts my head up to stare into his eyes. I gulp when I see his eyes have gone black with lust. He leans down and crashes his lips onto mine. His tongue parts my lips. His tongue slithers into my mouth, and my tongue fights his for dominance.

He pulls away from me and we're both breathing heavily. "No blindfold it is. I warned you, little spawn. Going forward, I won't be easy on you." He lifts my arms up and takes off my shirt and bra. Proceeding to bend down, he pulls my shorts off my ass, sliding them down my legs. My legs are spread wide as he leans in and licks my folds, moaning with acceptance. Back to his full height, he picks me up and slams me on the table, pushing my shoulders back. I hear chains rattle as he grabs them, locking my hands tightly so I can't escape. I am bare ass naked, chained to a table.

He walks over to the other table, grabbing something off of it. I raise my head, trying to watch. He pulls his shirt over his head and fuck, this man's back muscles and tattoos—he looks like a god. I can't help how wet I am getting just staring at his sculpted body. Turning around, he has a smirk on his face, walking back over to me with what looks like a ball gag.

"Seth... I can't—" I start to say. But I am shut down with him already putting it around my head and pushing the ball into my mouth.

"Oh, you can, and you will. I want to see drool dripping down that pretty face of yours." He brings his fingers down my body, feather-light, causing chills everywhere his fingers touch. Fuck, I've never done this before. What if I can't breathe? What if this thing makes me look like a drooling dog waiting for the bone? He leans over the end of the table, diving face first into my pussy. His tongue plunges inside like it's his last meal. A moan escapes my lips. I swear he has a thing for eating coochie because he's done this several times.

He licks up my folds and sticks his large fingers inside of me, pumping in and out as he continues to feast. He stops abruptly and pulls up a knife. It's not a small one, either; no, it's the one he has used on me before. I thrash in the chains, trying to scream, but he smacks my ass so hard I whimper. He flips the knife toward him and plunges the handle in and out roughly, causing me to rock back and forth, moaning, and I hit my climax and cum all over the knife, making my body go limp. Pulling out the knife handle, I watch him wipe my cum off the handle, and still chained, he grabs my ankles, flips my body to my stomach carefully, putting me in the most awkward position. He pulls me up a little and arches my ass into the air.

Smearing my cum up and down my asshole, he plunges a finger inside. I try to fight him as flashbacks invade my mind that I really don't want. But he is too strong. He pulls out his finger, reaching down to my pussy. Of course, I am soaked again. I swear my body hates me because of how wet I am right now. It's telling him to keep going. He plunges his fingers back into me, thrusting in and out. Once he is satisfied with the amount of juices on his fingers, he repeats soaking my asshole.

I have drool and tears running down my face, and all he can hear is muffled whimpers. Then, while I am distracted with my thoughts, I feel a sharp pain in my ass, and I scream.

"You are such a good girl. Relax. It won't be as painful once you relax. I have a butt plug shoved in that pretty tight ass of yours, working to stretch you out. Don't worry, princess, my cock won't be in your ass tonight, but it will be soon." I'm crying harder now, snot coming out of my nose. He spreads my legs further apart, and I feel the table move with him getting on top. My ass is arched again, and he slams his hard cock inside of me, thrusting in and out. No, he wasn't lying. He is taking me hard. He grabs my hair and yanks my head back. My scalp is on fire.

"You feel so good. Your tight, delicious twat gripped around my hard cock." He thrusts harder and harder, hitting my G-spot. I'm going to cum again if he doesn't stop.

"You are mine, Regan. Do you understand me? No one touches you." I nod my head as best as I can, since he still has my hair in his hold. He rocks my world longer, and I cum all over him, not once, but twice, and then he takes deep, slower thrusts and spills his seed inside of me. My body slumps against the table as he pulls out and pulls his pants back on.

He unhooks the chains and cradles me to his chest as he carries me out of his lair. We are silent as we enter his room, a million thoughts running through my head. It was him, the masked guy who took me. Who, even though I screamed and kicked at him, felt familiar. I wasn't scared of him and enjoyed the pleasure. Maybe this is the final sign from the universe that we were destined to be together.

Seth sits me on the toilet in his bathroom, holding one hand on my shoulder to keep me from falling forward, and starts his bathtub. This tub is HUGE, which makes sense given how damn tall he is. He adds bubbles and bath salts to the tub, checks the temperature, and turns back to me. He kneels in front of me, fingers touching my face, brushing strands of hair away.

He kisses my forehead and looks me in the eye. "I meant it when I said I will always protect you. I'm not letting you go again, baby girl."

I nod, trying to find my voice. "Why didn't you tell me it was you? Why would you kidnap me, take me disguised?"

He breathes out unsteadily, reverting his eyes downward. "I was going to tell you when the time was right. I saw you with Damon at the cafe, and I about lost my shit. I didn't like seeing you with someone other than me. That night, I knew I had to have you. You had to be mine. Damon is not trustworthy, and he was getting to know you to get to me for some reason. I don't know. I had to mark my territory. It's a shitty way of doing it, but I had to. You need to stay away from him, Regan." His eyes are pleading with mine.

I keep silent as I'm trying to process what was just laid in my lap. He picks me up again and sets me into the steaming bath. My muscles instantly relax, and I tilt my head back, shutting my eyes. I hear a zipper and clothes hitting the floor. When I open my eyes, Seth is staring down at me, observing me, waiting for my okay to join. I move forward as an invitation, and he steps in right behind me, lowering himself into the bath and pulling me to his chest.

I lean my head back and take in the smell of the oils. My head rests on his hard chest, his hands going up and down my arms, trying to soothe me. I close my eyes and take it all in, like my mind can finally settle. I went from loving this man when we were kids, to hating his guts, to crawling on my hands and knees to his beckoning call.

I feel him lean into my ear, his hot breath tickling the side of my neck.

"I love you, Regan."

Chapter 25

REGAN

Those words, "I love you", run through my head on repeat. Did I imagine them in the heat of the moment? Were they real? Where do we stand? He says I'm his, but do I want to be his? Yes, I do. So why am I questioning every little thing? Last night, he took care of me after our interaction. Well, adventure, adrenaline, and hot sex. My heart had raced; the fear was addicting. I want more and more. I could die the way he took me and be content with my death.

My phone rings, snapping me out of my thoughts. I look down, seeing Alex's name. "Hi, Alex! Yes, I am okay. Yes, I'm alive. Yes, I miss you!" I laugh, already knowing what she wants.

"Am I that predictable? It's like you know me or something. Glad to hear it. I'm coming over and we're having a girls' night. I have all our favorite snacks, and I got your fave! Dr. Pepper!" She's speaking a mile a minute, and I wonder if she is breathing at all. "Plus, Seth thinks it's a good idea!"

"Did you really ask Seth if you could come over like he's my parent? You do know I'm not a child, right?!" I snort, shaking my head.

"No, I told Cole that I really wanted to see you and that I miss you. He said he'd talk to Seth and make sure y'all weren't busy. He also gave me his key card so I can get up to the penthouse. I'm fully aware you are big bad Regan, who needs no man's permission and can handle things herself. I'll be there in twenty minutes. Love ya!" She hangs up before I can even respond. Sighing, I throw my phone onto my bed, walking into the bathroom.

I throw my hair into a messy bun and begin washing my face. Hands wrap around my waist, hot breath breezing against my ear. "You are so beautiful, baby girl." I jump, spinning around, throwing a punch toward the person behind me. My fist is caught mid swing. "Woahhh there, sniper. I didn't mean to scare you! I thought we were over the fighting!" Seth chuckles, letting go of my fist.

"Seth, I am so sorry. I was just startled, that's all. We aren't fighting, I promise. You can't sneak up on me like that!" I blew out a breath I didn't know I was holding.

"There is no one in this house except the two of us. Who has you so scared that you jump like that, baby? You know, I won't let anyone hurt you." Seth's eyes darken with concern. Those beautiful, dangerous eyes bore into mine.

"Alex is coming over for a girls' night. I hope you don't mind. We're just going to watch movies, eat junk, and talk about girl things. Wanna join?" I smile sweetly at him, changing the subject.

"No, I have to go to the club and handle some business. I'll have my men stationed downstairs. You ladies have a good night," he huffs and kisses my forehead. He turns, walking out of the room as I stare at him. I mean, really stare at him. He's so handsome, strong, and in his own way, powerful. Oh, God, I have fallen for Satan himself.

About twenty minutes later, Alex comes flying through the elevator door, arms full and a big ass smile on her face. I rush over to her, grabbing bags out of her hands before they fall all over the floor. Walking over to the counter, we set all the bags down and she starts to unload all of her goodies. Frozen pizza, ice cream, Dr. Pepper, cookies. Anything you can think of, it is in there.

Looking at me up and down, she says, "So, how are you feeling? You look... happy. Which, I am not complaining, but spill the tea. Why are you happy?"

"Considering I'm healing and haven't been hit by a car again, I'm feeling good. As for happy, things are definitely interesting." I can feel my cheeks flushing red. I go into detail about the events that have occurred. About the masked man, who ended up being Seth, our intimate encounters, and how confused I am, but also how I am falling for him.

"Regan! I didn't know you were a freak! I fucking love it. As for your feelings, let goooooo! Stop worrying. Seth has changed. He's still an asshole, but he's your asshole, who will do anything for you but also make you a little freak! Bring down that wall and let him in." She pokes me in the chest, giggling.

She's right, I feel safe with him. These walls need to come down! We spend the rest of the day gossiping, eating junk, painting our nails, and watching movies. It's getting late and both of us are curled up in a ball on the couch. Alex is passed out, and I begin to doze off when the elevator dings. I shoot up from my comfy ball and look over to see Cole and Seth walking in. They look around and their eyes go big with all the junk food and Dr. Pepper on the counter.

"We will clean it up. Sorry about that." I get off the couch, walking past them, when I feel hands wrap around my waist. He spins me around, brings his hands to my face, and kisses my lips gently. A shiver runs down my back. He pulls away with a smirk on his face. I blink a couple of times because I cannot believe what I am seeing. But I stop myself, taking it in. We head over to the kitchen and he helps me clean up the mess.

Alex stirs awake, sitting and stretching out like a cat. She heads over to Cole to give him a deep kiss. They are so damn good together.

"So, tomorrow night my parents are hosting a dinner at six. You both are going, so you need to go shop for dresses tomorrow," Seth informs us as he is putting the snacks in the pantry.

"Why are we going if it is your family's dinner? I don't want to intrude on a family event." I look down as I wipe up the counter.

"Shut up, Regan. What she means is we would love to go. How fancy do you want us for this dinner?" Alex is shooting daggers at me. She never gets to go to fancy dinners or interact with the Elders, so she will take every opportunity to see what all the hype is about.

"You are not intruding on my family dinner. I invited you. They want us to bring our girls with us, so why can't we show off our beautiful women? Your parents will be there, Cole's, as well, and some other Elders. So, like I said, you and Alex will need to go get new dresses tomorrow morning. Oh, and Regan, wear something red." Seth and Cole walk out and into his office that I forgot he had, shutting the door.

Alex stayed the night, sleeping on the couch with Cole, so it would be easier to wake up early and head over to this cute boutique. Slipping out of bed, I take care of my needs, wash my face, brush my teeth, brush my hair, and apply light makeup. I walk into my closet and slip on some jeans and a cute tank top, apply a necklace, and spray myself with my favorite perfume. I slide on my sandals, grab my purse, and head out of the room.

The smell of bacon and eggs hits me as soon as I step out of my room, making my stomach growl. The boys are in the kitchen cooking, as Alex is sitting at the island drinking orange juice. I didn't even know the boys knew how to cook.

Alex looks over at me, whistling. "Don't you look like a yummy snack!" she chuckles and eyes Seth.

He looks over at me and his eyes go big as he drops the utensil and walks over to me. Pulling me close. "You look beautiful." He takes a whiff of me and groans, planting a kiss on my lips. "Hungry? Grab a plate and eat up. You ladies have an appointment in thirty minutes, and we will be dropping you off." I chuckle and head over, sitting next to Alex, and dig in.

We pull up to the beautiful boutique and the boys walk us to the doors. "Here is my card; pick whatever you want, but make sure it's red. The color is perfect on you." He kisses my forehead and heads back to the car. I tuck his card into my purse. Staring off in his direction, my emotions begin to stir, as I was not expecting him to pay for my dress.

We walk in, being greeted by the store manager, who leads us over to our reserved area and dressing rooms. After we put everything down, we advise the manager of the styles we prefer and colors. Instead of going with a tight red dress, I go with a spaghetti-strap dress that goes to my knees. It's tight at the top, with a V cut at the neck, has a lacy top, then fans out at my torso. I also take back a couple of other long ones, just in case they are more elegant. I head to the dressing room once Alex has picked out her dresses and we begin trying them on. We have a few hell no's to the dresses and a few maybes.

It's so nice hanging out with Alex, trying on dresses, laughing and joking like we used to back in high school. I have really missed her. I finally put on that dress I originally wanted and stare at myself in the mirror. Instead of a bright red, it is more of a maroon, deep red. I look so beautiful. It's been a long time since I've felt confident. I step out of the dressing room to show Alex when I hear a gasp.

"You look breathtaking, Regan. Seth is going to love this on you, and maybe off of you at the end of the night." She fans herself. My face becomes so red when the manager nods her head and fans herself, too. The manager holds up a finger and walks away for a second. I scowl at Alex for that comment in public. The manager comes back with strappy black heels that match the dress beautifully.

Alex picks a beautiful tan-colored dress, which is surprisingly elegant and not as tight as I would have expected of her. She looks absolutely beautiful in the dress, and Cole will absolutely have that thing ripped off of her when they get home! We head over to check out, and Alex pays for her items and they wrap everything up and place it in a cute bag. I walk up and hand over my items, and then I look at the total. I about have a heart attack—three thousand dollars. My eyes are basically bugging out of my head.

"Girl, stop; you know they picked this place knowing how much we would spend. You don't have to say it, but I see your face." She grabs my purse, pulling out Seth's card and handing it to the lady. I feel so horrible spending his money, and I will definitely work extra to pay him back. They wrap up my items, handing the bag over to me.

I check my phone for the time and realize that we are going to be running late if we don't get out of this store and back to the penthouse. Alex tells me Cole is two minutes away to pick us up. As we head to the front, I am not paying attention and almost run straight into someone.

"Will you watch where you are going? Jesus. Oh, Regan, it's you." Morgan, the last person I want to run into, is eyeing me up and down.

"Hi, Morgan. If you'll excuse me, we have places to be." I try to push past her. She has been after Seth since we were kids, and I really don't want to think about their relationship while I was gone.

Chapter 26

MORGAN

Sipping on coffee across the street at the cute coffee shop, I see Seth's truck pull up to a boutique. Awe, maybe he is getting his mother something, or me, for that matter. I keep watching as I see him get out of the truck and almost spit my drink out when I see Regan get out with Cole and Alex.

What the fuck is she doing with him? I hit her with my car and swore I got her out of the way. The bitch just won't die, will she? Last I heard, she was in the hospital with serious injuries. I didn't think she would look, well, normal like she does right now. My coffee cup is slammed back on the table in frustration, wanting to scream but also not wanting to make a scene in front of the people around me, or worse, Seth, if he hears and sees me. I watch them carefully as they head to the door and Seth stops, kissing Regan on the forehead.

Seth never did that with me. The only thing I was to him was arm candy and a good fuck. I need to get this bitch out of the picture so I can have my man back, but this time, make sure she's taken care of. Fully aware that the guy I met up with had said not to kill her, but he won't know that it wasn't a freak accident.

I watch as Seth and Cole drive away and the girls enter the shop. How the fuck can they afford anything in that shop? Unless daddy is paying for it. I get up from my seat and head over to the boutique to see what these girls are up to. I enter the boutique and the bell rings, but no one comes to greet me. Normally, I would be pissed, but today, I don't need someone interfering with my spying.

I hear giggling toward the back and hide behind a rack when I see the two girls. "You look breathtaking, Regan. Seth is going to love this on you, and maybe off of you at the end of the night." My ears go on fire from what I just heard. Oh, so she is seducing Seth into keeping her around. Good to know. To think that he is inside of her, spilling his seed, when that is meant to be inside of me, makes my blood boil.

They head back into the changing rooms, and I go back toward the front, acting like I am looking at items. They head over to pay for the skanky clothes they think are good enough for the boys. As they walk toward the front, Regan is not paying attention and I step in front of her. She nearly runs into me. Stupid girl, no wonder she was easy to hit with a car; she doesn't pay attention to her surroundings. This may be easier than I thought.

"Will you watch where you are going? Jesus. Oh, Regan, it's you." I sneer at her, looking her up and down.

"Hi, Morgan. If you'll excuse me, we have places to be." She tries to go around me, but I step back in front of her.

"Why in a hurry, dear? Not like Seth is waiting for you to come to him like a stalking, pathetic little girl," I say, chuckling.

"If you must know, Morgan, Seth and Cole are waiting for us. In fact, they bought us these dresses for tonight." Alex, Regan's best friend, speaks up, trying to make her presence known.

"Oh, that's cute, considering he is coming to my house and my bed to fuck me tonight. He is probably going to leave you waiting and desperate." I chuckle. He isn't coming to my house, but she doesn't need to know that.

"Actually, he is taking us to his parents' house for dinner, where our families are going to enjoy each other's company. Bless your heart, Morgan. I know you are full of shit, considering he has been by my side. I would love to see you try to keep him from me, considering that he came right back to me once I got home. Have the day you deserve." Regan shoves my shoulder as she walks past me out of the door.

I could rip her back by her hair, and it takes everything in me to stop myself. I can't make a scene here, but I will have my revenge. That stupid little bitch has no idea who she's fucked with.

Seth Kingsley is mine, and she will learn that soon.

Chapter 27

SETH

After dropping the girls at the boutique, Cole and I head over to the ring shop. Even though she has no idea about our marriage, I do plan to tell her and not keep this lie from her. I want to make sure I give her the ring she deserves, as well. That way, she will be so impressed she won't say no. Well, the deed is already done, and there is no way in hell I am letting my little spawn have a choice to run. She may stab me, though, and that will just turn me on, especially seeing the fire in her eyes.

My palms are sweating, heart racing, and I am a little dizzy. I shake my head. What the hell is this? I hate this feeling. Feeling like my shield is slipping, all because of her. I wipe my hands on my pants and get out of the truck.

Pausing, I take a deep breath and pull the mask back up before Cole notices my slip. He's already out of the truck before he saw I had my moment of weakness. Thank God because I would not hear the end of it, and he would use that moment against me any chance that he got.

Walking into the shop, the bell rings when the door opens. This jewelry store has been around for decades. My father came here for my mother's ring, and my grandfather came here for my grandmother's. Oscar became the shop owner after his father passed away. I have known him my whole life, considering he is my father's childhood best friend. I refuse to go to the flashy ring shops when I can come to a shop that has meaning, history and pure heart.

"Hello, Oscar. Thank you for having us on short notice." Walking over to him, I shake his hand. He slaps me across the top of my head and pulls me in for a hug.

"Stop thanking me, Seth. Next time you try to act professional and uptight, with that handshake with me and this fellow again, I will remind you where you learned your ways and make you tap out like you did when you were a boy," he says, tilting his head back and laughing. Old man's still got it and can make even an eight-foot man feel small.

"Now, I hear there are congratulations in order. What kind of ring are you looking to get my beautiful niece? Will she be attending dinner tonight?"

"Thank you! There's just a little problem, though." I look up from examining the rings.

"Hmm. It can't be all smooth sailing, can it? What's the problem?" He eyes me suspiciously.

"She has no idea we are married yet. She will be at dinner, so all I ask is to not mention anything. I want to smooth the news out with a perfect ring." I take a deep breath, preparing for the scolding to start.

"Your reasons for making that decision—were they for your own gain or to protect her?" he asks, tapping his fingers on the counter while waiting for my answer, with his eyebrows shooting up to his hairline.

"I would never do anything for self gain when it comes to her. I have to protect her," I answer honestly.

"Then I won't say a word. Your sister will be proud." Coming around the corner, he grabs me in a bear hug for a brief moment and heads back around the corner.

I advise of her ring size and cut I had in mind. We spend the next several hours looking through the different styles and colors. Oscar has the biggest smile on his face and doesn't take my rejections or suggestions to heart. He is actually pleased that I am being very picky. It means, to him, I am serious and taking into consideration the styles SHE would like, not what I would like.

Cole gets a text from Alex letting him know that the girls are ready to be picked up. He heads out as I stay behind a little longer. Just when I thought about giving up and coming back another day, a ring catches my eye and happens to be Regan's size. It is perfect for my little spawn.

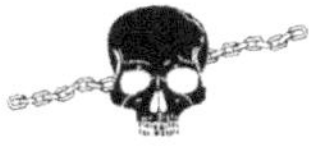

Music playing throughout the house, I walk out of my closet, putting my red tie on. I purposely chose red to match Regan's dress, wearing a black button-down dress shirt, black slacks, and shiny black shoes. My choice of appearance really does give me the Satan stigma. Glancing at myself in the mirror, I make sure my tie is even and center. My black hair is slicked back, tattoos peeking up my neck and hands. Brushing off a piece of lint from my shoulder, I grab my suit jacket and shrug it on. I spray my best cologne that smells smoky with a hint of leather.

My eyes are looking down when I walk out of my room, and I look up as I enter the living room and lock eyes with the most beautiful person I have ever seen. Regan's legs look long and muscular in those tempting heels. My eyes go up her legs to her torso, up her chest, and finally meet her eyes. She is mouth watering. If my mother wouldn't kill me for not showing up, I would keep her home and do some dangerous things with her in that dress.

My eyes are lit with fire as I prowl to her, catching her by the waist. "You look incredible, my little spawn." I take a whiff of her, and she even smells so fucking good; lavender and vanilla invade my senses. My mouth is watering, needing a taste of this dangerous demon who could easily put me on my knees.

Her cheeks flush red, looking down in embarrassment. With my forefinger, I tilt her chin up. "Keep that chin up high—own the self-confidence. You are a fucking goddess that deserves to be worshipped." Leaning in, I brush my lips against hers. "I'll gladly get on my knees for you tonight." She gasps, grabbing her hand as I lead her to the elevator, and I can feel her eyes on me. Her eyes roam my body. I smirk and the doors close, descending to the truck.

We pull up to my parents' house, fancy cars lined up at the entrance. Cole and Alex pull up next to us, blaring music. Cade is sitting in the back seat of their truck, clearly the third wheel. Regan's parents are here, along with several other Elders and an unknown car I don't recognize. Getting out of the truck, I walk over to the passenger side, opening the door. Regan exits, taking my hand, and we head toward the entrance with the two lovebirds and Cade trailing behind.

The door flies open before I can even touch the doorknob. "Seth, I am so happy you finally made it." My mother swallows me in a bear hug. Letting go of me, she moves over to Regan. "My dear, it has been way too long, and I am so happy to have you here with us tonight." My mother's eyes twinkle, pulling Regan in for a hug.

Once my mother finally lets go of my girl, we walk through the doors. My parents' butler takes my suit jacket, and we head into the dining room. My dad stands from the head of the table and greets us, along with Regan's father and several other Elders.

Pulling out a seat next to me, Regan slides into the seat, murmuring a thanks. As I go to sit in my seat next to my father, a male walks in. My body freezes when I see Damon strolling in with a cocky smile on his face. What the fuck is he doing here?

"Seth." Damon nods over to me after shaking my father's hand. "Regan, it's so good seeing you again. I haven't heard from you since I saw you at the club." His eyes skim up and down her body, causing my blood to boil.

"Damon, what are you doing here? Sorry to burst your bubble, but she is with me. Unfortunately, there won't be any other dates moving forward." Feeling my rage rise, I feel a hand on my thigh. I feel myself start to simmer down with a possessive high. That small gesture was all I needed.

"I would appreciate it if you didn't look at me like a piece of meat. That is why you didn't get a second date," Regan huffs, turning to Alex, giving Damon a cold shoulder. That's my girl.

"I had business to discuss with the Elders that doesn't concern you. I happened to be here, and they invited me to stay for dinner. Is that a problem?" He arches his eyebrows, turning and walking to the other end of the table before I'm able to answer.

Looking over at my father, he leans in. "We had questions about his relationship with his grandfather. Something wasn't adding up. He will stay and have dinner, but we are keeping an eye on him. We will discuss further once we have answers. Now change that look on your face before your mother kills us both."

We carry on the night discussing memories, laughing at each other's jokes, and discussing trips we need to make in the future, like we did when we were kids. Our moms sure know how to get all sentimental and shit, but with how happy they are and their smiles, I didn't have the heart to try to interrupt their ramble. Plus, I think I am more scared of my mom than I ever will be of my father.

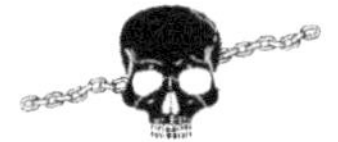

Regan

Besides the awkward encounter with Damon at the beginning of dinner, the night has gone smoothly, and surprisingly, makes me feel like the old days: free, safe, and home. Glancing over at Seth, he has a spark in his eye—smiling and relaxed. I haven't seen him like this in a very long time. I can't help but feel my heart warm at the sight.

"Regan, I have to say you are glowing. I am assuming you are feeling better from your accident. I'm so happy nothing heavy happened!" Mrs. Kingsley reaches over the table, taking my hand. I love her so much. She has always been so sweet.

"I definitely feel a lot better! Thanks to Seth. He has been very caring, making sure I went to my follow-ups and felt better." My cheeks redden as he slips his hand onto my lap.

"I am so glad you are back in town, and especially with Seth. He will protect you and make sure you are put on the highest pedestal. We raised him that way. With that being said, congratulations are in order for you two!" She raises her glass and everyone follows her lead.

I look over at Alex with a confused look, and she shrugs her shoulders. Seth tenses next to me. What the fuck is going on?

"To our newlyweds! We are so happy to have you part of our family finally! We have always adored you and have been waiting for this to happen. Although, I wish it was a big wedding for us to attend." Instantly, the room goes quiet. Mr. Kingsley is shaking his head. Seth is frozen.

"I'm sorry. What did you just say?" My heart is racing, eyes popping out of my head, hands trembling.

Her face drops, cocking her head to the side. "We know you didn't tell people due to everything going on, but we are family in this room. No need to be shy!"

Seth yells, "Mom!" at the same time his dad exclaims, "Dear!" My mind starts to spin. What the fuck are they… then it hits me. Did he do what I think he did? Son of a bitch. He didn't have the courtesy to ask me if that is what I want. I may have said yes with the way I fell so hard for him once again.

Pushing myself from the table, I murmur, "Excuse me." I hurry out of the room. The feeling of passing out creeps nearer with each step. I need air. Panic rises as the need to get out of here grows more intense.

"Regan." I hear Alex behind me, but I ignore her and go out of the front door. Tears streaming down my face, I can't breathe. I'm halfway down the driveway when a large hand grabs my arm.

I twirl around, facing Seth. "Regan, let me explain." Without thinking, I slap him. I shove him away from me, but his hold is too strong.

"How could you, Seth? You took this away from me. You took my fucking choice away from me. And your parents knew? Do my parents know? Did everyone in that damn room know EXCEPT ME?" I scream at him.

"Regan, stop! Breathe. I had to do it. I had to make sure you were safe. Being married to me will keep danger away from you. No one will cross me, cross my family. I was going to tell you tonight after dinner. This was supposed to be a surprise with just the two of us. I didn't know my mom knew. The only people who knew were my father and your father."

Of course, my father knew and couldn't tell his own fucking daughter that he was marrying her off. I'm a wife, and I didn't even have the chance to be happy about it, to say yes, to call my best friend and giggle like schoolgirls. The experience of signing the papers, glowing with happiness was ripped away from me. I didn't get the chance to be happy that I finally got to marry the person I have wanted since we were kids.

Now I am just pissed, hurt, fuming, and I want to stab him. I just might at this rate.

"Please listen to me. After what happened to you, and what happened with the Wolves, all I wanted to do was protect you. I wanted to make sure that it was me who was tied to you. It was me as your protector and savior." He is shaking, like his life is being ripped from him. Good, because that's how I feel right now.

Thunder cracks above us and rain starts to downpour as we stand in the middle of it.

"I don't need a savior, Seth. You aren't God. You can't control every aspect of the world and what will happen. Do you understand that? I am not a weak female you can push around. So, you did this out of pity. I get it." I throw my hands up in the air and push past him.

"I'm okay being made into the villain. I never said I was perfect, but I do know that I didn't do this as a pity, Regan.

I did this because I love you and I need to protect what is mine." He twirls me back around, and I nearly trip into his arms.

"Do you, Seth? Because if you loved me, you wouldn't lie to me and keep this from me. I have loved you since we were kids. I loved you when you broke me and I decided to leave this shitty town. I hated you over time. I forced myself to hate you. You were the enemy, ready to destroy everything in your path. I fell back in love with you before I even knew it, when you took me from Alex's and forced me to live with you. I would never do something like this, ever." Tears run down my face. The way he is looking at me now, he is about to trap me back in his sticky web.

"I'm sorry. I shouldn't have done it the way I did. At the time, it felt like it was the right thing to do. But I swear on my last breath, I will never keep things from you. There are things I can't tell you with the Wolves, but involving you and me, I will not keep anything from you again. I swear on that. I have you now, and I can't lose you again." His hands cup my face, his piercing eyes staring into mine.

"I will get on my knees and beg for your forgiveness if that's what it will take." He lowers himself to his knees, holding onto the side of my legs, looking up at me. Who would've thought I would have this dangerous man on his knees? How can I stay mad at him? How can I knock someone down who was trying to do what he thought was right, especially being raised by an organization who has the final word and decision?

"Get off your knees, Seth. No more lies. Do not make huge decisions that will affect me without my consent. I have had enough of people making decisions for me. I might actually stab you." I take a breath and slowly release it.

He stands up, towering over me, leaning in and kissing me. He pulls away and leans into my ear. His breath against my ear makes me shiver. "I promise I will let you stab me, my little spawn."

He pulls something out of his suit jacket and gets on one knee. Opening the box, a ring shines in the moonlight. "Regan Marie Dale. I know it is already done, but will you be my wife?" My hands are shaking uncontrollably. I nod my head yes. "I need to hear you say it."

"Yes, yes, I will already be your wife." I chuckle, and he stands, sliding the most beautiful ring I have ever seen onto my finger. It is a cushion cut, with a black center diamond and regular diamonds around the black diamond. It is a perfect fit. Cheers fill the driveway, hooting and hollering. My cheeks burn red, and I pull Seth in and kiss him.

I am a Kingsley. Well, I guess I have been, but now I officially know I am a Kingsley.

Chapter 28

Unknown

I received a text earlier advising of new information that was obtained about my dove. Meeting at the spot we agreed upon, I wait impatiently for him to arrive.

Hearing the door creak open, the guy walks in, holding a folder in his hands.

"What do you have for me?" I eye the folder in his hands.

"Regan was involved in an accident. My sources say she was hit by a car. I'm still looking into if it was an accident or intentional." Opening the folder, he hands over photos of Regan coming out of the hospital.

"She's been living with Seth Kingsley in his penthouse. She is heavily guarded at all times." Why the fuck is she with this guy? Who the fuck is he to her?

The next sentence causes me to freeze. "Also, I have discovered that she is married to Kingsley. He used his connections for the legal paperwork to be completed on the down low, preventing anyone from stopping it. She seemed to have no idea this had occurred until later."

Rage takes over my body and I slam my fist into the wall. This is going to cause a bigger roadblock than I anticipated, but nothing is going to stop me from getting what I desire the most: her. She'll be punished for his little act.

"The Wolves have an assignment coming up that I know they'll send him on. I don't have more details, but I know he is due for one. Once he is gone, I'll capture her and bring her to you." He steps toward the door, ready to leave.

"No. You'll keep an eye on her, track her movements, and schedule. Advise me of where I need to go. I'll get her myself." Walking over to the table and grabbing a rag, I wrap it around my bloody fist.

"I also want an update on the woman you brought with you last time we met. She has been quiet and has not reported anything back to me. I want to know what she is up to."

He nods in acknowledgement, disappearing from my sight.

Pulling my phone out of my back pocket, I send a quick text to my men to get the cell block ready.

She can hide behind a Wolf, but that won't be enough to keep me from her.

Sitting on an iron chair, I stare into the abyss, listening to the *Tick. Tick. Tick.* from the clock on the wall. Grabbing a knife, I make slashes on my arm. The fragment of pain consumes me, but also makes me feel powerful. I swipe a finger through my blood, walking over to the wall. I trace an image of a birdcage on the wall.

Soon, sweet bird, I will have you back in your cage.

Chapter 29

SETH

I feel awful about the way Regan found out about the marriage. Of course, my father doesn't keep things from my mother, or she snooped and squeezed it out of him. But he failed to tell her to keep it quiet.

We get home and I don't waste any time moving her into my room, where she belongs. Throughout the next week, I help her move her clothes into my closet and let her go crazy organizing everything. I can tell she is still hurt, but she looks down at her ring often and a smile stretches across her face.

My mind drifts back to Damon. Why the fuck was he at my parents' house? And then the look that he had when we returned to where our family was all crowded, making an excuse that he had to leave. That didn't sit right with me.

My phone vibrates in my pocket, and I pull it out, seeing that Cade set a text.

> **Cade: I was able to locate a video from Regan's accident.**

> **Me: Meet me at the club in 20 minutes.**

I send a quick text to Cole to meet us at the club. Grabbing my jacket, I walk over to Regan and kiss her forehead.

"I'll be back in a bit. I have to run to the club and take care of some things." She nods her head and goes back to organizing. She's in her cleaning mode, and I am not going to disrupt that. I head out of the penthouse and down to my truck.

I arrive at the club and head inside. Heading up to the office, I get out of the elevator and find Cade and Cole already sitting at my desk.

Cade gets up from the seat, motioning me to sit. I sit and lean into the computer. Hitting play, I see Regan coming out of a tea shop with a smile on her face, when a little boy comes up to her, handing her a bag. They exchange words, but I can't hear what was said. The little boy runs off in a hurry.

Regan opens a note, and I notice her facial expression changes when she opens the bag. It looks like she screams and drops the bag. She steps backward and gets hit by the car, which speeds away. Looks like it was a setup. Rage is running through my veins. My body is vibrating, flipping the keyboard and throwing a glass at the wall.

"Who is this kid? We need to find out where this bag came from and why it made Regan terrified and nearly lose her life." Pacing back and forth, my heart races.

"I have located the kid and questioned him with his parents. He said some hooded guy gave him twenty bucks, showed him a picture of Regan, and told him to give it to her. He didn't know who it was, and when he ran back over to the hooded guy, he was gone," Cade confirms, nodding at the computer.

"I think we need to go to the hostages in the basement and get some answers. They have to know who it is and how we can find them," Cole suggests, getting up from his seat and heading to the door. The hostages are still alive. Barely, but we feed them enough so we can still get answers from them.

We head down to the basement, and my first reaction is to stab these idiots, but I need answers.

"Wakey, wakey." Cole throws water on each hostage. They groan and shake their heads.

"What do you know of Regan Dale and who is after her?" Pacing the floor in front of him, I can already feel my patience running thin.

"You mean the pretty little redhead? We don't know shit except that she is your little side." I punch him in the nose before he could finish his sentence.

"Not the answer I'm looking for. I will ask again. What do you know of Regan Dale and who is after her?" I walk over to the table and pull pliers out, then head back over.

"We don't know shit about your little redhead." The man spits on my shoes. I grab his hand and rip a fingernail from his finger with the pliers. He screams in pain. I go to the next guy and do the same. I do this until all but one nail is taken from each. These fuckers aren't giving up.

I go back to my table and grab a knife. I walk over and slit the Achilles' heel of each of their left legs. They scream louder, begging for me to stop, blood pooling underneath them.

The man on the right cracks first. "We don't know who it is. We never got a name. He's part of the Snakes, but he was always hooded and wore some sort of mask, so we couldn't see what the guy looked like. I remember her mentioning something was taken from him and he wants it back. He had us watch and locate her movements, but then we got an assignment at the warehouse where you took us from. We don't know anything else from there."

"Shut the fuck up, you idiot," the one on the left spits, and I don't miss a beat and stab him in the chest, digging the blade, twisting, pulling it out, and he slumps, dead. A sinister grin spreads across my face as I turn to the last living hostage.

"Look, man, I just did what I was told. I told you everything I know. Let me go! I swear I won't talk. I swear I'll disappear." This sleaze is begging me. He thinks I am going to let him go. What a stupid, stupid little boy.

"I'll do you a favor, and I'll make it quick." I pull my gun from the back of my waistband. *BANG*. I fire the gun and blood covers the floor, the wall, and my clothes.

Regan

I spent the last couple of hours putting clothes away in the closet, taking a shower, and snuggling in bed, watching Netflix. Seth had Wolf business, so I have no idea when he'll be home. My eyes start to feel heavier and heavier, and I slip into a deep sleep.

My body is shaking, bruised, and battered because I made him angry again. I had too much cleavage, he said, and too many men were looking at me. He never hits me in the face because it will cause too many questions from the public.

His fist connects to my stomach, and I double over in pain. Tears run down my face, snot coming out of my nose. He pulls out a blade and kicks me over onto the ground. He rips my shirt off, and I am begging him to stop. I plead and plead, telling him that I'm sorry, but he isn't listening. He takes his knife and cuts deep under my breast, and I scream in agony. His laugh is sinister as he pulls the knife away.

I try to scramble away, but he pulls me by the legs, sitting on top of me and pinning me down. He pulls a syringe out of his pocket and slams the needle into my neck as I scream. I instantly go mute. I'm screaming, but no sound is coming out of my mouth. My body goes numb and I can't move.

He yanks down my pants along with my thong. He smacks my pussy, pulls down his pants, and pulls out his cock. Why is my body failing me? What did he do to me? I can't move. I don't want this. Please, someone help me!

He gets between my legs and slams into me, taking me forcefully. He takes me over and over again. Once he is done, he flips me over and slams into my ass. I can feel liquid down my backside. I can feel the pain, but I can't do anything about it. He gets off of me and pulls his pants up.

"You look so pretty with blood smeared all over you. My little dove has color to her white feathers." He walks over

me, leaving me on the floor and slamming the door behind him.

I wake up screaming, with hands on my shoulders. I fight and kick, trying to get them off of me.

"Regan, it's Seth. I'm here, baby girl, you're safe." My eyes flutter open as my body vibrates, trying to catch a breath. Tears stream down my face. "Shh, it's okay. I'm here." Seth has me on his lap as he is rocking back and forth.

He doesn't ask right away. He lets me cry into him as the trembling takes over my body. The tears begin to lessen, as there are no more that can possibly come out of my eyes. I am numb. Reliving my nightmare is terrifying, and what is more terrifying is that HE could find me and do it again and again. It'll be worse the next time he gets me because I stabbed him and ran away.

I know I have to tell Seth. He's going to know this wasn't a normal nightmare. He needs to know because if something happened to him, Alex, or his family, I wouldn't be able to forgive myself.

Pulling away from him, I take a deep breath. "The scars you asked me about. I lied about how I got them. I didn't come home because my father forced me, or because I wanted to. Coming home was something I had to do in order to be safe."

Seth's eyes darken. "What do you mean, you came home to be safe? Safe from what?"

"When I was at school, I met someone. He was nice for a while. He treated me right, and I thought that I could put the Wolves, my family, this place, behind me. But after a while, he changed. He became possessive about what I wore, who looked at me, and where I went. He dictated everything I did. The more time went on, he started hitting me. Places where people wouldn't notice.

"He would drug me, rape me, torture me. I thought I was going to die. For a time, I prayed that he would just get it over with and just kill me. He cut me under my boob because I was wearing a shirt that showed too much cleavage. Then he would stab me with a needle, injecting a substance into me that made me mute, and I couldn't move. He raped me and left me on the ground, where I laid in my own blood." Saying these memories out loud makes me shake all over.

"He did other things to me that make me want to vomit. One day I snapped. I woke up chained, stabbed, and exhausted. He walked in and let me out of the chains so I could freshen up for some event he had. I took the opportunity and grabbed his knife, stabbing him, which allowed me to escape. I already had a suitcase packed under my bed. It was ready for when I had a chance to escape. And then I came home."

I look up at Seth, and he is already on his feet, pacing back and forth. If looks could kill, his would this very second.

"The first threat I got, I don't know if it was him. The second threat, I knew it was. He called me his little dove. I got crows—dead crows—sent to me, which symbolize death." Looking down at my hands, I feel better telling him my secret, but I am haunted that this man is going to come for me and kill everyone I love.

After a few minutes of silence, which feel like hours, Seth kneels down to me. "Who was the one hurting you, Regan? What is his name? I promise you, he will never hurt you again. I will find him and I will kill him."

"His name is Jackson O'Brian. Though, I don't know if that is his real name because I learned he had so many secrets and he was involved in some heavy gang or club. I don't know. I'm sorry I didn't tell you. I didn't want the people I love getting hurt. If they started threatening my family, friends, or you, I would surrender myself so you could live." Tears prick my eyes as I look toward the window.

"The hell you would. I will never let you go, Regan. How stupid would you be to go back to the pit? You would be killed as soon as you got there. I won't let that happen. Do you understand me? I will burn this fucking world down so that YOU can live." He pulls me into his arms, kissing my forehead. He takes a deep breath, another, and then another.

He pulls me up to the bed, and I snuggle into his chest. I take in his smell, and it comforts me. It reminds me that he is my safe haven. He is my home. We stay like this for the rest of the night—neither of us talking, neither of us sleeping. Not for a while, anyway.

At this moment, I fall harder for this man. He didn't punish me for keeping this from him. Nor did he leave me. He reassured me that he will end Jackson so that I can truly live.

Chapter 30

SETH

It's been a week since Regan revealed her secret to me. I have worked endlessly, trying to find Jackson O'Brian and who this jackass is, but I can't find him. He is a ghost. It's driving me insane. She gave me details on what he looked like, a rough area on where he lived. He kept his home a secret from her, as he blindfolded her every time he took her there. She only calculated the minutes from her dorm when she counted on the way there.

The place she ran from was not where he stays; she knew that for a fact. I have the boys looking into it as well. I'm both exhausted and also aggravated that we can't find this ghost. I have doubled the security for Regan for when I'm not with her. The best of the best, so nothing slips by.

Taking the next few hours away from our search, Cole, Cade, and I sit at a jazz club to have a few drinks. Stepping away may help us clear our minds, but really, I needed a stiff drink.

"This guy has to be part of the Snakes or some other group because there is no way an ordinary guy covers his tracks this well." Cade throws back his whiskey, slamming his glass on the table.

"He is good, but we are better. He better pray to whatever god he worships that we don't find him." Cole mimics Cade, throwing his whiskey back.

"How is she doing, by the way?" Cade eyes me from the other side of the table.

"She is having nightmares more frequently, or maybe I notice them more now that she is in my bed. But I won't let anyone or anything harm her again." I take my last sip, feeling my body burn to take out this aggression on someone. I never wanted to kill someone like I do now.

One of the waitresses comes up to us with another round of drinks. We didn't order another round. "Sorry to bother you, but I was advised these are for you. They said you look like you need them." She places the drinks down and walks away.

"Who sent the drinks?" Cade shouts after the waitress.

She looks around the club, trying to locate the mysterious person. "Looks like she left already."

Cade shrugs and picks up his drink and takes a sip. Cole and I do the same and change the subject for the rest of the night.

As the night goes on, I start to feel weird. I become dizzy and my body starts to become numb. What the fuck? Did I drink too much? I look over at Cole and Cade, and they look equally fucked up and then pass out right then and there. My eyes get heavy and I lose consciousness.

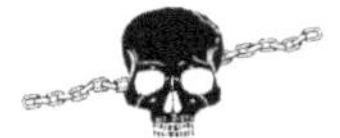

I wake up to my phone going off. I rub my face and sit up. It's 9 p.m., and hours have passed, and we are back in my office at the club. Fuck, it's late, and how did we get here? Cole and Cade are still passed out on the floor. I go to grab my phone and see that Regan has been blowing me up. I quickly sit up, thinking something is wrong.

My hands are shaking. I get up, kicking the boys awake, and throw my phone at them. How the fuck did this happen? I walk over to my desk and click on the computer. I skim my surveillance; the idiots didn't even think about wiping it out.

There are hooded masses dragging us up the elevator to my office. I click the next screen to my office and see we are placed carefully. Another slender woman walks in wearing a red robe. She pulls down her hood and what do I see? Morgan, half naked. She lies next to me, posing for the pictures she sent to Regan.

"I could kill her. I know it is frowned upon to kill a female, but I don't give a fuck." Cole flips over the couch as Cade rubs his face, trying to come out of his daze.

I grab my phone back and upload the videos and send them to her.

Me: Baby, just watch the video.
I promise you it's not what you think.

I make a phone call to the club owner and disclose that it appears we were drugged and I want the waitress fired before I do worse.

"We are going to pay a little visit to this whore and bring her back to Regan so she can decide her punishment." I walk out of the office with the boys at my heels.

My truck tires squeal when we get to Morgan' house. Heading up the stairs, I kick open her door. The lights are off and it is so silent, you can hear a pin drop. Cade goes through the rooms and advises it is clear. She is nowhere to be found.

Cole is typing erratically on his phone and looks up. "I can't trace her phone. It's like she disappeared. I have another guy working on what he can find."

No one drugs me and gets away with it. I am fucking pissed and take a vase from the table and throw it against a wall.

After dropping them off to their trucks, I walk into the penthouse to Regan pacing across the living room floor.

"She better have a good fucking hiding spot because when I catch her, I swear I will fucking end her." My little spawn is fuming, and it instantly turns me on.

Walking up to her, I push her against the wall with my hand wrapped around her neck. "I like this side of you. You see how hard you make my cock. Don't worry, my little spawn, she is all yours." Before she can say a word, I capture her mouth in mine. Her mouth parts as I slither my tongue against hers.

She fights me for dominance. Gripping her neck harder, pinning my body against hers, I push her into the wall. I pull away from her mouth and she is breathing heavily. Licking the side of her face and down her neck, I clamp my teeth down and mark her. She cries out in pain, but then a moan quickly follows.

Gliding my hand down her shorts, I find my naughty girl isn't wearing underwear. Stroking her clit, she quickly wraps a leg around my waist. I slip a finger into her already soaking pussy and slowly slide in and out, adding another finger, going harder, rougher.

"Stop teasing me, Seth, and fuck me like it's the last night you live." She moans in my ear.

I turn her around to face the wall, bending her over. "Both hands on the wall, and spread your legs like my good little slut." She shivers and does as I say.

Pulling down her shorts, I reach under and rub her soaked pussy again. She is spread out, waiting for me to take her. My cock is so hard it hurts. I can't play around like I want to. It springs out of my pants, ready to penetrate that sweet tight pussy. I bend at the legs because she is so short and I am so damn tall. I grab her by the hair and yank her head back.

"I want to hear you beg me. Beg me to ruin you." I nip at her ear.

"Yes, Seth. I'm yours, ruin me. Take all of me, just get inside of me." That's all it takes as I shove inside of her, still holding strong on her hair. I see her eyes roll back, and she screams in pleasure. I pull out of her to the tip and slam back into her over and over again. She is shaking, trembling at the knees. Good.

Slamming into her hard and fast, she cums all over my dick, but I still have it in me. I take and take and take until I cum inside of her. Pulling out of her, she nearly collapses as I catch her and carry her to our room. Laying her on the bed, I head into the bathroom and get her a warm washcloth. I clean her off, pull her under the covers, and slide into bed.

"That is a reminder to never question my loyalty, Regan Kingsley. I am yours, and you are mine." I kiss her forehead as she nods her head and slips into a deep sleep.

I could do this all night, over and over, just to remind her where I stand. That pretty ring on her finger is not just for show. It is a promise.

Chapter 31

SETH

It's been three weeks since the incident with Morgan. She hasn't shown her face in town, and we can't track her location. She's a ghost. This raises my suspicion that she is involved in a lot more than the pictures and sabotaging my relationship.

We haven't had any leads on Jackson, either. It has been quiet, which I'm not complaining about, but it just seems to be too quiet. Regan hasn't received any new threats, so we are still trying to figure out if the two threats are from the same person or separate, especially with everything going on with the Wolves.

I received an assignment last night from the Elders. They got a hit on the location of a possible lair for the Snakes. We are being sent out in the next couple of weeks to scope it out and see if we can find any information, or if the head of the Snakes is there. We have strict orders to take out anyone who gets in our way except the leader. He is to be brought back alive.

I don't want to leave Regan here alone, but I don't have a choice in the matter. My father and hers are aware of the threats and will have heavy security with her at all times. Alex will also stay with her while we are gone. Regan wasn't happy about it, but we had to tell our fathers what happened to her. She didn't think her father would give a shit either way and would blame her, but to our surprise, he was as enraged and ready to take down the son of a bitch as much as I am. But he will have to fight me to have the honors to kill this prick.

The club has reopened now that we don't have any hostages lurking in the basement, so I agreed to let Regan go back to bartending to keep herself busy. She needs it, too, because she is driving me insane with her constant pacing back and forth at the penthouse. We go in together and leave together, and I monitor her from my office with the cameras to make sure she is safe and that no one coming into the club tries to harm her.

Everything between us has been amazing. We are definitely learning each other's ticks, especially when her Dr. Pepper is gone, and she knows I drank her last one. I swear she was going to throw the knife at my head.

I have a huge surprise for her tonight. Honestly, we both need it and to get out of the city.

"Seth, where are we going and why am I blindfolded?" My little spawn is being impatient, grumbling in the passenger seat.

"We're almost there—be patient. Has no one ever done surprises for you before?" I chuckle, looking over at her.

"You said that twenty minutes ago. I hate surprises; everyone knows that. Hence why I don't get surprises." She folds her arms across her chest, scowling.

I make a right, driving up a long driveway that has a canopy of trees lining the sides and surrounding area. We reach the end of the driveway about five minutes after the turn and come to a stop. I put the truck in park and get out, rounding to the passenger side. Opening up her door, I take her hand and lead her out of the truck.

"Put those hands down and don't touch that blindfold. Be a good girl and listen before I punish you. Keep your hand in mine and I'll guide you." Kissing her forehead, I lead her to the front.

"Bossy asshole," she mutters under her breath. I smirk. Oh, she will get it later for that sly comment.

We get to the front steps, and I let go of her hand to take off her blindfold. She takes a second to adjust her eyes and looks around in confusion.

I hope she likes it because this is our forever.

Regan

Seth takes off my blindfold, and adjusting my eyes, I look around us. Sitting in front of us is a massive two-story house. It's white with black shutters, has steps to a deck with a wrap-around porch and a bay window. There are double doors leading into the entrance of the home. Vines creep up the massive home and trees surround us as far as I can see. I am so confused. What is this place?

"Seth, where are we? I don't understand." Looking at him, I catch the huge grin on his face.

"We needed a change of scenery and a home that can be called ours. Not the penthouse, that was just mine before you moved in." He hands me a set of keys and gestures to the door. "Your name is on the house, too. You own it. Stop gawking at me and go inside. I had the house furnished already, and all we need to do is move our clothes in."

Grabbing the keys, I take the steps two at a time. Unlocking the door, I gasp at how beautiful the gray wood floors are. The walls are a light gray with white trimming, and it is massive. Walking further into the house, I see two offices, and an open concept kitchen with an island—a beautiful, large kitchen, may I say. There is the family room with a TV that is almost as big as the wall, gray fluffy couches, and the walls are lined with beautiful artwork. There is another open room with a pool table and a bar area.

Upstairs, there are five bedrooms, and the master bedroom is enormous. Walking into the bedroom, there is a California king-sized bed, and there are two walk-in closets. One for him and one for me. Thank goodness I don't have to share. I could have a whole bed in here if I wanted to! It even has an island in the middle with drawers.

The bathroom has a beautiful deep garden tub, a walk-in shower, and double sinks. I take the next hour exploring the house. I don't think we need this big of a house, but I'm not going to complain because he put so much thought and work into this house.

I walk downstairs, still in a daze, imagining our future, having our friends come over for dinners and playing pool, having family gatherings and living in peace.

"What do you think?" That gorgeous, muscular man leaning against the island says, staring at me with a hint of sparkle in his eyes.

"It is perfect, quite spacious for the two of us, but perfect." I creep slowly to him, trying to be seductive but probably looking extremely awkward, and I almost tripped on my own feet. Awkward.

"Good, this is meant to be our safe place, our home. There is a basement—the door behind the bookshelf will lead to it. In there are all our guns, safe, and everything you need in case I'm not here. It's there to protect you." Jesus, this man just keeps adding and adding. It doesn't surprise me, though, with it being hidden and full of weapons.

Next thing I know, his hands are wrapped around my neck and he brings his mouth crashing down on mine. My lips part, inviting his tongue in. I love the taste of him. He tastes like mint and he smells like old spice and leather.

He pulls away from me, leaning toward my neck, his hot breath against my ear makes me shiver. "Get on your knees and open your mouth," he growls. My eyes go wide, and I slowly drop to my knees. Not fast enough, as his large hands push me down by the shoulders.

"Be a good girl and open that pretty mouth of yours. I want you to choke on my cock as I fuck your mouth." My legs clench as I feel myself become wet instantly. I do as he says as he undoes his belt and unbuttons his pants, pushing them halfway down. His cock springs to attention.

I knew he was bigger than normal, but I never had it in my face like this. He is massive with his piercing, and there is no way that thing is going to fit in my mouth.

He grabs me by my scalp and shoves himself down my throat. This man isn't gentle, and I'm already gagging. His hips begin to thrust into my mouth, and I take him.

"I want one hand holding my cock and one touching that pretty little clit of yours. I want you soaking, ready for me." A moan creeps out of my mouth, and I grab his cock and stroke as my head bobs up and down his shaft. I reach down into my pants and rub the tips of my fingers in a circular motion against my folds, sliding in a finger, and then two, pumping in and out.

He moans as I take him, and he thrusts into me deeper and harder. His body vibrates and he cums in my mouth, pulling out once every drop is seated on my tongue, clogging my throat. "Swallow it, all of it," he demands. And I gladly do it.

He pulls me up, bends me over the countertop, pulling his belt from his pants. He wraps the belt around my neck in a tight grip. I can still breathe, but damn, it sure makes it hard.

He rubs my folds with his tip and slams into me, causing me to scream. He thrusts in and out, nearly banging my head into the countertop. "You look so pretty when you are bent over as I take what is mine. Tell me, little spawn, do you love this as much as I do?"

I can barely speak as he rails me hard, holding his belt in a tight grip. He slaps my ass, causing me to jump. "Yes, oh God, yes. Don't stop," I scream.

"I am the only god you will worship," he growls.

He pulls out, thrusting his fingers inside of me, causing me to cum all over. He pulls his fingers out and smears my cum over my asshole. My body tenses, and I freeze.

"I will claim you in every hole. Relax." He lets go of the belt and it drops to the floor, replacing his hands on my scalp. He pulls back my head and licks my face.

Sliding his tip into my hole, I feel a sting. He pushes himself deeper and deeper, and I cry out. He does one big thrust and I don't even think he's all the way in. Tears running down my face, he slips his hand between my legs and thrusts two fingers inside of me, pumping in and out. He starts to move and pumps himself into my ass, deeper and harder, keeping up with the motion of his hand.

Moans escape as he goes faster and faster into both holes. Then we are both tipping over the edge, finding our release together. He pulls out and I slump over. He pulls up his pants, picks me up, and takes me upstairs to our new room. Walking into our bathroom, he sits me down on the edge of the bath as he turns on the water and adds oils and bubbles. I love how he pampers me after he makes me sore.

Carefully, he lowers me into the bath, undresses, and slides in behind me.

Leaning up against him, my eyes fall closed. He wraps his arms around me, kissing the top of my head. "Welcome home, baby."

Chapter 32

SETH

Hidden behind trees and tall grass, we wait and watch. The cold breeze howling around us reminds us we have our wolven spirits watching, protecting us for what is to come. The smell of swamp fills our noses, with croaking of the frogs filling the night's silence.

Dressed in black head to toe, with our wolf masks tightly pressed against our faces, hidden from prying eyes, we wait for what seems like days as we watch the tattered house for activity. It's the perfect house for a lair, as any average person would think it's an old abandoned house, dying from mold and critters.

The house is a worn down two-story with window shutters hanging off the hinges, overgrown weeds that come to my middle thigh, a wrap-around porch with rotting steps leading up to the entry, and old rusted chairs sitting on the porch. Just looking at the chairs, I feel like I will need to get a tetanus shot—or five.

"Do you really think this is the right place? I mean, there hasn't been any movement, and we have been sitting out here for hours," Cole whines as he slaps himself on the arm, killing a bug.

"You sound like a little bitch right now, Cole. How did you even get into the Wolves?" Cade glares, looking him up and down.

"Fuck you, man."

"Will you two shut the fuck up? You will get us discovered if there is anyone out here," I snarl at the two grown ass men arguing like they are in middle school.

After another thirty minutes, the night sky's growing darker and darker, and I signal to move forward to our destination. We have our guns raised; we creep closer and closer. There are no vehicles to be seen and no lights in the house—silent as the dead. Slowly, I move up the creaking porch as the boys have my back and sides.

Turning the handle to the front door, it's locked. I get down and start picking the lock until I hear a click, then I whistle, letting them know I got it. Creeping into the entrance, I take the hallway down until I see a room to my left. Monitors fill the walls, along with a desk with keyboards, papers scattered on the desk, and three chairs. I clear the room and head to the next.

When the house is cleared of any presence, we investigate the rooms, finding beds upstairs, bathroom needs, and trash piled up in a trash can next to the counter in the kitchen. There are definitely signs of people staying here.

We head to the bigger room with more monitors displayed and a Snakes leather vest sitting on the chair. Humming of electricity fills the space. One thing is for certain: this is a Snake's lair, and will tell us what they are monitoring. I head over to the monitors and click them on. Bright lights shine in the dark room. One by one, they click on, displaying our warehouse, different locations of our town, and inside our church. How did they get in there? We would have seen them, and it's guarded.

Moving to the next screen, I find shipment schedules, guard rotations, and notice they figured out a gap. Moving to the wall, articles from years ago line it. Looking closely at the pictures and dates, I realize that this was my initiation assignment. Why would they have this?

Mark McAllister was last seen at his brother's home. Nobody found, no traces of where he is located.

Looking at the picture, I signal Cade and Cole over to take a look.

"That's the guy that I killed during our last assignment the Elders sent us on. He was one of the brothers." Cole reads the article, confusion on his face. Why would the Snakes give a shit about a judge and the brothers?"

Walking out of the room, I find a hidden door in the paneling that leads to the basement. I whistle, signaling the boys to follow. Guns raised, we open the door and head down the steps, taking it slowly so we don't make any noise. Empty. I find the light switch and flip it on, causing a red glow throughout the room.

Entering the space further, I notice photos hanging from a string and a mural on the wall. I pause, eyes widening when I notice they are all photos of Regan. There are photos of her at her parents' house, picking up a box with a scared look on her face. Another with her picking up and reading a note.

I travel to the next cluster of photos of her in the bar, working and smiling at customers. A photo of her walking out of the building to the penthouse, the coffee shop she was at, and entering a tea shop.

The next is a child coming up to her, handing her the package. The next one shows her lying on the ground after she got hit. What sick fuck thinks they can stalk my girl and keep these photos of her being threatened? My body is shaking with rage. These fuckers are too close for comfort. Where the fuck are they now so I can rip their heads off their bodies and feed them to the gators?

"Seth, over here. They have a photo of Regan and Alex at the boutique we took them to. Is that Morgan I see? What the fuck is all this shit?" Heading over, I look to see the girls walking up to the doors to leave and Morgan walking toward them. Something catches my eye, and I walk past Cole. On the wall are more photos of Regan in different places, with a mural on the wall. Some are new, but some look like when she was beaten and bloody before she came home.

You may have flown away from the nest, little dove, but I will find you and put you in the cage where you belong. I'm coming for you, pretty bird.

Reading the print in the middle of the mural, I lose my shit. I roar, flipping tables, throwing a chair across the room. Shredding the photos off the walls, fists flying. I see red, and I am ready to go to fucking war.

"Seth, calm down. This is sick shit, but we need you level-minded." Cade drags me up the stairs. Cole is on the phone, making calls to the guards at my house.

"Guys, we have a problem. No one is answering, and the video feed to the house is cut. We need to leave now." We race out of the house to the truck, piling in, foot slammed to the floor.

Cade is on the phone with the Elders, alerting them to what we found. My heart is racing. We have a four-hour drive to get to the house. My pretty little spawn better be tucked safely in bed. I grab my phone, dialing her number, but get no answer.

"Answer the fucking phone!" I howl.

Chapter 33

REGAN

Seth is gone for an assignment. Where? I have no idea; I am not allowed to know. But he assured me that this place will be guarded and safe while he is gone. Alex stayed over to keep me company in this big house.

Music blasting, we dance around the house in shorts and tees like we're in high school, taking advantage of our parents being out of town. We played a couple rounds of pool, made pizza, and took a couple of shots of Crown. Once we had settled down, we cuddled up on the couch and put a scary movie on.

As the movie goes on, thunder suddenly cracks and shakes the house, causing us to scream. We look at each other and giggle. Rain starts to downpour on the roof, making more of a spooky vibe with this scary movie.

Lightning cracks and the power goes out. We look at each other, eyes wide. Okay, that is creepy. Shadows pass the windows and I gasp, rubbing my eyes. This movie has me really on edge and seeing things. The front door squeaks open, and Alex and I hit the floor. I scramble for my phone, realizing my phone is sitting on the counter. Fuck.

Whistling fills the room, coming closer and closer. My heart is racing, beating filling my ears.

"Come out, come out, little dove." A deep voice echoes through the room. No. No. No. He's found me. How did he find me? Looking over at Alex, I put my finger to my mouth, signaling her to stay quiet. We crawl around the couch, peeking around the edge. I see him go into one of the rooms, and I signal for Alex to run up the stairs. She does and makes it to the top of the stairs, stopping with her eyes wide as I am getting to the middle stairs.

A hand wraps around the hair at my scalp, yanking me and throwing me down the stairs, and I hit the floor. A cry flies from my lips as I hit my back hard, knocking the wind out of me. I open my eyes to the monster standing over me, and a scream rips out as I'm pushing myself backward, away from him. A terrifying laugh fills the room.

Alex darts down the stairs with an object in her hand, hitting him so I can get away. He doesn't even flinch. He turns around and throws her into the wall, and she crumbles to the floor. I get to my feet and dart toward the kitchen, aiming to grab a knife and get over to Alex.

Large hands grab the back of my head and slam my head into the counter. My eyes cloud and I fall to the ground. As I come to, blood dripping down my face, he grabs my legs and drags me around the counter. I kick and scream, trying to fight him, but his hold is too strong. It's like kicking a brick wall, staying intact while I crumble.

He starts humming a tune as he slides me across the floor to Alex. She comes to and grabs onto me, shaking.

"Please, let her go. She has nothing to do with this, Jackson," I beg, as Alex holds me tighter.

He whistles, pacing in front of us. "Now, where would the fun be in that? Poor little Alexandra will suffer like you, little dove." He laughs, causing my heart to drop to the pit of my stomach. "Two pretty white birds smeared with crimson blood. What a pretty sight.

"You have five seconds to get up and run. If I catch you, you are mine. One."

We scramble to our feet, running up the stairs to get away.

"Two."

We hear him slowly coming up the stairs. We head into the guest bedroom, and I signal her to the closet.

"Three."

I close the door to the closet and open up a trap door I found while exploring the house. I signal her to go in.

"Four."

I hear him getting closer and closer. She slides in, and I follow, closing the door.

"Five. Come out, come out, wherever you are." He laughs. Tears running down my face, I can't breathe. How is he here? I hear a knife being dragged against a wall.

"I will find you. And once I do, there will be no escaping. Not even the Wolves can protect you," he yells out.

I hear him in the closet. Please don't let him find us. His footsteps fill the silence—searching, hunting for his prey. As the footsteps disappear, a loud sob escapes from Alex's mouth. The sound of hangers separate and the locked doorknob rattles. We hold our breath, hoping he moves on, but then the door flies open and his face appears.

"There you are." He grabs me by the neck, yanking me out. He pushes me against the wall, pinning my arms above my head. Alex comes barreling out, jumping on his back, trying to pry him off of me.

He spins, and she is thrown to the floor. I make a run for it, grabbing a vase and throwing it at his head. He side steps and walks over to Alex and punches her in the face, knocking her out cold. I run to the bathroom, trying to find something to defend myself, and he comes running up behind me, shoving me into the mirror as it shatters into my scalp.

Grabbing me by the neck, he squeezes. I grab his hands, trying to yank him off, but he only goes tighter. There are scissors on the countertop, and I grab them, swinging and stabbing him in his side. He lets go, and I cough, taking off out of the room and down the stairs. I need to get to the basement for a weapon. I barrel down the stairs with him hot on my heels.

"You bitch. You will pay for that!" I don't stop or look back. As I get to the bottom of the stairs, he supermans through the fucking air, landing on me.

I scream. I can feel my ribs cracking, my air being cut from me. He picks me up and throws me against the wall. He walks over, pulling a knife from the back of his pants. Holding up my arm to block him, he cuts my arm. I moan in agony. My body hurts.

Before I can register his movements, something hard hits me in the head. My vision blurs, and the last thing I hear is that dark, demented laugh. The world goes black. Please tell me this is the end.

Chapter 34

SETH

Blood is rushing through my ears. My heart is racing, causing me to lose my breath. I am zipping in and out of cars, earning me the blaring of horns. Please, please be okay.

Both Cole and Cade have been at it on their phones, trying to get ahold of the girls and trying to get the cameras back up. They notified Regan's father, but he too is hours away for a regional meeting. Where are the guards? They can't all have dead phones.

I can feel it, even though I keep begging whatever god is out there. I know they are in danger. Beating my fist on the steering wheel, I wonder how could I be so stupid and leave her? After all the threats, I still left her alone.

Lightning cracks across the sky, booming thunder filling the silence. Turning at the next exit, we are so close. I hit gravel and press down on the gas. Rocks hit the side of the truck as rain pours down around us. It's a sign. Nothing good is about to be discovered.

When we pull up to the house, everything is pitch black. Lights are out, no sign of life. There are no candles lit or flashlights shining against the window. We come to a screeching halt, and I jump out of the car, sprinting toward the house with the boys close behind me. I come to a dead stop when I get to the door.

Two guards are leaned up against the front door, blocking the way. I flash on my phone light and step back.

"What the fuck!" Cade stares in horror.

The guards are slumped together, facing forward, and obviously dead. My stomach sinks as I take in their faces. Their eyes are pinned open, and smiles have been carved from their lips up their cheeks. Above them, on the side of the house wall in blood, is a message.

The smile of the Wolves that fall.

My hands shake. I push them over and kick down the door. I barrel inside, not even bothering to check if it's clear.

"REGAN!" I roar, hoping she hid herself. Entering the kitchen, I hear a crunch under my feet. I shine my light and see glass is covering the floor. Looking over, I notice blood on the countertop.

Taking two steps at a time up the stairs, I yell for her again, but there is no answer.

There's more glass, more blood tracing the walls. Fuck, no. I wasn't fast enough. My fist goes flying into the wall, causing a massive hole.

Rushing down the stairs, I almost run into Cole.

"The rooms down here are clear. I haven't found either girl." Cole's body is trembling with rage. "We need to find them. If they took Regan, they took Alex, too. Both of their vehicles are here."

I race toward the basement, where I showed Regan to go in case of an emergency. The emergency lights flicker on. But there is no sign that anyone was down here. They are gone.

"Seth. Cole. You gotta see this. They have them," Cade yells from upstairs.

Entering the room that Cade is in, blood lines the walls.

Out came the Snakes and killed off all the Wolves. And the little bitty birdie goes up in flames again.

This sick fuck turned the itsy bitsy spider rhyme into a war message. My rage takes over as I flip furniture, grab a knife from the kitchen, and carve the message out from the drywall. I feel nothing but fire in my veins.

Stepping outside, I roar Regan's name, falling to my knees, and punching the ground until my knuckles are bloody.

Fight, Regan—stay alive. I am coming for you.

Acknowledgments

I know this is cliche, but I want to start off by thanking my mom. She has taught me to be a strong, driven, independent woman. She always supports me when I chase my dreams or knocks me across the head if I ever doubt myself. When I was too afraid to write, stressing over others' opinions, she sat me down and gave me a heart to heart. She is my rock, my backbone, and I don't know where I would be without her.

I want to thank my amazing PA Bethany Smith. We met online talking about books, and the next thing you know, she became one of my biggest supporters. Dealing with my emotions, reading through my work, giving pointers, and also becoming one of my long distance besties! She has her hands full being a mama, building her own empire, and still took time out to help me! I appreciate you so much! I am proud of you!

Cassandra Elizzabeth! I started out on her street team, overly obsessed with her book Love Eternal! I mean so much so that as I was reading, I would message her with my WTF moments! When I decided to write, she was so quick to dive in and help me with tips and tricks, where to publish, who to go through for edits, and so much more! She is the absolute sweetest, and I may have gone mad without her help! Thank you so much!

Thank you to my readers for taking the chance by picking up my book and reading. Without you, where would the book community be? Where would I be without the love, support, and hype? The spicy babes, who aren't afraid of being feral!

Lastly, but not the least, my fiancé. He knows I have an over-obsession for reading. When I decided to write, without any second thought, he told me to do it. He would listen to me ramble about ideas, cry from frustration, and then talk a million miles per minute about plot twists and the spice. Although he isn't a reader, he told me once my book is done, he would sit down and read it. That's a lot, especially from him. He has been patient with me while I sit countless hours writing and editing and never once complained! Love you, hubs!

About the Author

Satan's Spawn is B.L. Swern's debut novel to the Empire of Wolves series. She resides in Arizona with her partner, son, and two dogs. When she isn't writing, she is out with the family riding the Razor at the dunes, camping, going on adventures, and buying way more books than needed. Her favorite books to read are Mafia, Dark Romance, Fantasy, and anything Witchy. Make sure to check your sanity at the door when reading her book and prepare to clench your legs!

Make sure to follow her Instagram, TikTok, and Goodreads!

www.ingramcontent.com/pod-product-compliance
Lightning Source LLC
Chambersburg PA
CBHW040859010826
48978CB00013BA/1086